Mama's Baby
Daddy's Maybe

Written by:
Qualo Lowery

Cadmus Publishing
www.cadmuspublishing.com

Acknowledgments

This book would not have been possible without first and foremost "GOD;" He was who guided me when I didn't knew anything about the book business and how to write a book. I would like to thank Betty Brown, "AKA BIG MAMA" for supporting me through the last 17 years, and putting up with my mess. Next, I would like to thank my mother Brenda Blackmon and my father James Silas, without them it wouldn't be a me. A special thanks to my brothers and sisters, they provided me with laughs about my nieces and nephews through this whole process. Thanks as well to Andrell Bolton, Rhonda Norris, Nikki Smith, and Arlena Grier. I told all of you that I was going to get this book in print, my dream is here...I would like to thank my kid's ZZ, Shaquala, Jaquala, and Qualo Jr for letting me come back in your lives. Last, but not least I would like to thank everyone that purchased this book from Authorhouse. Thank You. Thanks to S.W.I.P. Foundation, Da Rossi Project. Thank you Cadmus Publishing.

I can't forget about Julian Sawyer who was my ears and eyes during this process.(He did the editing.) Shout out to my Dalton Village Family and my West Blvd Soldiers.(A special shout out to Tanya Thomas. You know how to spark my thought process. Thank you.) A super "Thank You" to the casting producer, Zack from the show" Love After Lockup." I'm looking forward to working with you! So is Tanya! My release date will be coming soon.

CONTENTS

PART ONE

PROLOGUE

RHONDA

Year: 1998

I was eating ice cream in my new two-bedroom apartment when I noticed the mailman making his way over to the neighborhood mailboxes. My armpits and hands were sweating from the anticipation of the arriving blood test results. This test had been taken by my current boyfriend Jay. I had asked him to take the test because I had a semi relationship with this guy name Martez when Jay and I were having problems. Martez had agreed to take a test too, but he decided to wait until I saw the results from Jay's test.

It had been four weeks since Jay had taken the test. The whole time Jay and I were waiting on the results, we were constantly at each other necks. One minute we were like a happy married couple, then the next minute we were on a mental roller coaster. I felt like our relationship was similar to Ike and Tina Turner's relationship.

We had decided that we would be together even if the baby wasn't Jay's. Jay was already acting like he was the father. This didn't shock me because I knew how much he wanted to be a father. He had told me that he wanted to be a father because his father wasn't there for him when he was a kid. I respected Jay for this and I prayed that he was the father of my child.

I put the pint of ice cream down on the table in my living room. Then I made my way over to the front door after I slipped into my purple bedroom shoes Jay had purchased for me for my 18th birthday. I had looked over all the baby stuff that Jay had purchased before I walked out to my mailbox. The gray hair, slim-built black mailman was getting into the jeep that he had pulled up in when I walked outside. He waved to me as I opened the mailbox. I waved back after I pulled out the test results. I was interrupted by Jay's car system as he turned into the neighborhood parking lot. I quickly put the small test results inside my pocket and then turned towards Jay.

He met me with a smile. I smiled back. I was faking but I knew Jay was happy because he wanted to be a family man. He didn't know I was still in love with Martez and I didn't want to be in a relationship with him. The reason I didn't tell Jay that I didn't want to be in a relationship with him was because I needed a man to be with me during my pregnancy. I didn't want to be alone. This was why I had lied to Jay when he asked me if I loved him. I had told him I loved him because I did, but I wasn't in love with him. I was still in love with Martez, but he was in love with someone else.

When Jay stepped out of his car, he asked, "Why are you not ready to go to your doctor's appointment fat-girl?" Jay knew I was super-sensitive about my weight. I responded, "I'm not fat. I'm just healthy."

Jay asked, "Did the test get here yet?"

I responded, "No."

I wanted to tell Jay the truth about the test, but I wanted to see the results first. This was why I lied to him. After I told him that the test hadn't come, I rushed back into my apartment and hopped in the shower. I had less than an hour before I had to be at the health department. I was going to the Health Department to get a checkup. There was a rumor in the street that Martez was carrying a STD. I just wanted to make sure that he hadn't given me a STD.

Jay dropped me off at the Health Department and told me to call him at his sister's house when I was finished with my check-up. I had lied to Jay about what I was getting a check-up for. I also convinced him that he didn't need to be with me at the Health Department.

RHONDA

Two Hours Later

I walked slowly toward the health department building after inspected my warm up suit and my blue matching Nike Air Maxes. There was a semi-forming crowd inside the lobby area of the building as I signed the check-in sheet. I recognized a pecan tan color young woman across the room reading a magazine, and she looked to be around five-foot-three in height with hazel brownish eyes. This female looked like the same female I saw get out of Martez's rental car the night I was looking for Martez.

I decided to approach the chick since I didn't get to say anything to her that night.

"Don't I knew you?"

The chick placed the Jet magazine down on the table in front of her then said. "I don't think you do."

This female had her gear together. She had on a cute Gap outfit with some sandals that had straps that wrapped around her calves.

"I do know you. I seen you with this guy I know."

The female said. "I'm sorry but I'm not really be out in the streets like that."

"I'm not trying to be nosey or funny, but do you know who your baby daddy is?"

The female shouted "Look here bitch!"

It was like this female's words had knocked the breath out of me. I wasn't use to being called a bitch. Especially in front of a crowd. I said "Who you calling a bitch. You the stupid bitch."

The female said. "No, I'm not the stupid bitch. You are. I know who you are. I saw a picture of you inside of Martez's rental car."

"You're mean to say my rental car I let him drive."

She said. "Like I said, you the stupid bitch."

The semi crowd turned their attention on this female and me. I could hear some of them saying things under their breaths. I said "I don't want to lip box with you. I came over here to talk to you about the situation I have with Martez. We can be women or we can be fools."

The female said "Martez told me all about you."

I hesitated then asked. "Oh, did he?"

"Yes, he said you work for him." She said.

I couldn't let this chick continue to shine like she was the sun, so I asked in a smart manner. "In which way?" The crowd gave me an approval like they understood what I was saying. Then this chick went into her ghetto attitude and said "Selling pussy and rocks."

I couldn't believe my ears. This chick was assassinating my character like I wasn't even standing there. I said "He played you like that, trick?"

She said. "What do you mean?"

The female was standing up now. We were about ten feet apart. I said "Martez told me you was just a dirty butt that holds his dope."

"Ha ha ha.. You are so funny. Martez is the father of my baby." She said.

This information was new to me. Martez never told me he had a kid or had a kid on the way.

"So you having Martez's baby?" I asked.

The female turned proper on me. She said "Yes. I'm six months pregnant and here for my check up."

There was a few Ah Ah... and some Ooooh ooohhh...

I couldn't let this chick out do me in front of this crowd. So I said "What a coincidence. I'm pregnant too. Martez is my baby daddy."

I gave this chick a fake smile. She didn't appreciate my fake smile because she still responded back with a disrespectful tone. She said. "Look here, I don't have time to be playing games with you."

"I'm not playing games. I'm really pregnant by Martez." Then I poked out my stomach to let her see the evidence.

I knew I was going out on a limb saying that Martez was the father of my child, but this chick was getting the best of me in our lipboxing match. I had to do something to even out the odds.

✦ 6 ✦

Chapter 1

RHONDA
Year: 1996
Time 4:00PM

I'm Rhonda Norris, a ghetto chick that was born in South Carolina but grew up in the city of Charlotte in North Carolina. Being 14 years old and being dumb to the street life had made me a victim to my first baby daddy: Dewayne. I had already been molested by one of my mother's boyfriends before Dewayne and I had sex. I found out I was pregnant the third time Dewayne and I had sex. This was three months later.

My sister Meke knew something was wrong with me after I had told her I missed my cycle for the third month in a row. She had told our older sister Tanika about my episodes of throwing up in our bedroom trash can. I didn't conceal these incidents or the fact I was pregnant when they told my mother. Yes, I was fucking, and I was enjoying the feeling since I had been raped the first time I had sex, and didn't know it was supposed to be enjoyed.

Several months later my daughter was born, and she was seven pounds with no birth defects. Her eyes were the same color as mine and she was dark skinned like her father. I was perplexed about Dewayne not being at the hospital when my daughter was born because he had promised me that he would be there. He lied. Just like a dead beat.

It didn't help that my mother had gone downtown and took out charges on Dewayne for having sex with me, since I was a minor at the time. He stopped coming around and disappeared from the neighborhood, all-together. This was after the cops had come through looking for him. The feeling of hurt had taken over my heart because I really thought he loved me but in the end, he just used me like my mother's boyfriend did.

The best thing happened to me after I lost Dewayne. I met Jay Morris. The day I had met him, I was walking down Fleetwood Street on my way to the neighborhood store. He was dressed in blue jean shorts, a polo shirt and Jordan's. He was the same height as me. His dark skin was what caught my brown eyes. When he called my name I almost swallowed my tongue. Then we made eye contact. Then he said, "What's up baby girl?" This baby girl stuff touched a nerve. I was now a woman since I had dropped a load. Going through the process of having a kid had taught me a lesson. And that lesson was motherhood was real. I said, "Don't call me baby girl. My name is Rhonda."

"Sorry Rhonda," Jay responded.

I gave him my ghetto look. I poked out my lips and rolled my eyes. He said, "I'm lacking at my game today. I hope you forgive me."

I responded, "Well I don't play games. Games are for kids."

He asked, "Where are you on your way to?"

I said, "I'm on my way to the store to grab me some tampons. It's that time of the month." I could tell this wasn't what Jay wanted to hear. In my eyes, he looked like another Dewayne. A liar, a cheater and a guy that targeted young girls to boost up his ego. I came to this conclusion after he had told me his age. He was five years older than me. Here I was, 17 years old with a newborn baby, no education and not a pot to piss in or a window to throw it out of. And on top of that I was addicted to sex.

I thought my comment about my cycle would have made Jay change his mind about chasing me but it didn't. He asked, "Can I walk with you?"

I said, "I don't care."

As I walked in front of Jay, I could feel his monstrous, hazel eyes running over my delicate physique. I was what you called a ghetto dime-piece. I turned around and asked, "What are you doing? Undressing me with your eyes."

He shouted, "No girl. I'm just checking out my new girlfriend."

I knew Jay was trying to boost up my ego. He didn't know I had been around the block a couple times. I responded, "I heard you got a girlfriend." I knew Jay was selling drugs and I knew he was fucking two other girls in the hood. I asked, "You got a girlfriend?"

"No I don't. Who told you that?"

"My sister Meke."

"She did?"

"Yes."

Meke had told me about how Jay was fucking all the other young girls in the hood. She also told me he tried to make a move on her. I said, "I have to think about if I want you to be my man." I didn't have to think. I knew I was going to make Jay my man the moment I saw him. As we got closer to the store, a black Cadillac turned on the street and started following us. Our conversation was interrupted by the car's music system. I noticed three black guys in the car. The one on the passenger side had large bumps, the size of sunflower seeds on his face. His braids were cornrolls to the back with rubber bands on the tips. The other two guys in the car had on black baseball caps and black t-shirts. I turned around when Jay said, "Hold this."

He reached me a stack of money wrapped in brown rubber bands.

I stuck the large knot of dead presidents in the pocket of my Daisy Duke shorts, then I turned my full attention to Jay as he said, "Run...run.." When I looked up, the Cadillac with the thugs in it was right on top of us. The passenger jumped out the car with a gun so long that it looked like a telephone pole. Jay shielded me from the thugs as they pointed their guns at us. I could see the fear in his eyes before I took off running. It was like three devils had arrived and Jay wasn't ready to go to hell.

I struck out towards my building. I was glad I had on my Air Max Nikes because I was going to wear my bedroom shoes but Meke had stopped me. The guy with the bumps on his face had taken off behind me. I was too quick for him. I was up the hill before he could get off a shot. After he had shot at me, I heard him say, "I missed the bitch." I ran as fast as I could to my building. Before I reached my building I heard Jay screaming. Then I heard several more gun shots...then I watched as the thugs sped off in the Cadillac. I could hear the tires spinning as they left the neighborhood. I turned towards Jay and ran back down the hill where he was lying on the ground. When I got to Jay, I noticed him holding his right eye. Blood was on his polo shirt and his new Jordan's were gone off his feet. He was shouting, "I can't see. I can't see!"

CHAPTER 2

MARTEZ BROWN
Place: Charlotte, NC...West Blvd.
Time: Evening. Light rain.

Selling drugs had become my life. I was born a natural hustler. The shit is in my bloodline. Looking back at my family tree, I found out that I had received this hustling trait from my mother's side. All my great uncles and great aunts were hustlers. They had sold moonshine and drugs ever since they were let out of slavery. They even did it when they were slaves.

I started selling candy in school when I was just seven years old. This earned me the nickname Money Man. That name didn't last long because my grandmother found out about me selling candy and made me stop. My life had changed when my mother left me with my grandmother when I was eight years old. There was no more fun and games. It was all business with my grandmother. She looked at me as a check.

I had overheard her and my mother fighting about the food stamps and the welfare check that my grandmother was receiving for me. This had made me feel like my parents didn't want me. My grandmother only took me in for the money. This had broken my heart, and I felt alone and used. When my grandmother had made the comment that I was only a check I felt like I had been cut to my soul with a spiritual knife. This made me perplexed about life. I had hate for the world.

I had always gotten the third degree from my grandmother when it came time for the yearly visit from the case worker. This was the lady that came by to see if my grandmother was using the welfare check right. My grandmother liked the money but she didn't like the white folks from the welfare office looking through her apartment. This always made her mad.

There were many rules that my grandmother had to follow in order to keep the 236 dollars and the three hundred dollars' worth of food stamps. Rule number one: Have a clean apartment.

Number 2: Evidence of how the money was being spent. Number 3: Proof that I had been going to school. Number 4: No drugs were allowed inside the residence. My grandmother was usually prepared for all of this.

I didn't like these rules the white folks at the Welfare office played by, so when I turned seventeen, I decided it was time to enter the drug game. It was like I had hit the lottery when I started selling crack cocaine. Everything changed. Like my clothes, shoes, women, and the people I dealt with.

I met my first real connect at a strip club. He was from West Blvd. He had fronted me the product I needed to set up shop at this junkie Val's crib. Two months into my operation, trouble came knocking. Three guys in a black Cadillac pulled up on the curb close to Val's house. "Put that damn pipe away." I shouted. Val took one more pull from the glass dick and put the glass pipe inside her house coat pocket. Then she walked over to the window and joined me. I could see three heads in the Cadillac.

"Who are those guys?" I asked.

"I think that's Chuckie. He be buying powder from Vest," Val responded.

Vest was this guy Val was messing around with before he had been arrested for a bundle of Boy. In other words "Heroin"

"He's probably looking for some powder," Val said as she walked towards the front door of the three-bedroom house. Since she knew them and I had a little bit of powder that I had stashed in Val's daughters' room, I didn't protest when Val requested for a gram of powder. I went to the room and retrieved the powder out a small brown teddy bear that I had cut a hole in the back of it, to stash my product.

"Here you go," I said to Val when I returned to the room. She put one of my fitted baseball caps on her undone hair and headed out the door. I really didn't understand Val. Especially, when she was smoking crack. It made me angry when I saw someone with natural beauty and smarts do stupid stuff. I knew that crack was taking over the way she was thinking, but I wasn't doing anything to stop her from doing the drug. She had already lost her kids to the state, because she had left her five-year-old son in the bathroom where the bathtub was full of hot water, and he almost lost his life due to her neglect.

I watched Val as she walked in the rain to the car. I knew what she was thinking. Like any other crack head, she was thinking about a hit. When she had reached the car, I noticed the guy in the passenger seat with a gun in his hand. Then I heard "BOOM... BOOM..." The sound had startled me. This sound wasn't new to me. I had grown up hearing this sound in the hood all my life. I grabbed my gun off of the table, then I ran to the front door. As I opened the door, I could hear car tires spinning. Then I watched as Val hit the ground. When I reached Val she was laying on the ground face-down. The rain was pouring down on her body, and I could see blood running with the flow of the rain water, rolling down off the pavement. I grabbed my weapon out of my pants and busted off a couple of shots at the car. There were people peeping out of the windows in the neighborhood now, but no one rushed over to help Val.

Val was struggling to breathe when I turned her over. I dropped the gun and rolled her on her back. I had seen so many of my homies shot and killed in my hood growing up that I knew not to move her. I just made sure she was breathing.

"Are you alright Val?" I asked as I looked into her brown eyes. No response. I noticed the blood on Val's chest area. I took off my jacket and placed my jacket under her head. Then I raced back to the house and dialed 911. I gave the operator at the police station my emergency number and the address to Val's house. Then I returned to Val's side. She was struggling to breathe. A lady who stayed across the street started walking over to the scene, but stopped when we made eye contact.

"Help Please!" I shouted over the falling rain.

"Is she dead?" the lady asked.

The lady was dressed in PJ's, bedroom shoes, and she had rollers in her semi-gray hair. Her skin was dark brown, and her eyes were the size of golf balls. The lady reminded me of my grandmother. She shouted "WATCH OUT!"

I moved out of the lady's way. Then I grabbed my weapon off the ground. Then it hit me. There was a possible chance that the police would want to search the house. I knew I had several thousand dollars' worth of crack cocaine vials in the house, and a stash of powder cocaine in the teddy bear.

I gathered my thoughts and rushed off to Val's house. Once inside. I went straight to Val's daughter's bedroom and grabbed the teddy bear. Then I opened the closet and grabbed the large bag of crack vials, that were stashed inside Val's teenage daughter's coat. Then I cleaned up the living room and took a seat.

I could hear the sounds of a firetruck coming up the street as I was sitting there waiting. My palms and both of my hands were dripping with sweat now. I could hear myself breathing like I just finished a high school track meet.

I decided to put all my drugs in a trash bag along with the

teddy bear. Then I put the trash bag with the items inside it in a large trash can behind the house. Then I put my gun under the house and returned to the crime scene.

A black detective had pulled up on the scene as the medical workers were struggling to get Val in a stable condition. The old lady that had helped me with Val was approached by this tall, slim, wavy hair detective as she broke loose from the crowd of medical workers.

I watched as he introduced himself to the old lady. Then I took in the sight of him pulling out a small notepad and start to taking down notes. I couldn't tell exactly what was being discussed, but I knew it was about the shooting.

The old lady pointed in my direction, as the medical workers finally stabilized Val. I didn't know what the lady said to the detective, but whatever it was, he turned his full attention toward me after he had finished with her.

I watched as the medical workers put Val inside the ambulance. Then as I turned to go back towards Vilas's house, I noticed a few crack heads were walking towards the house from the opposite end of Ross Ave.

I gave them an evil stare and a wave of the hand, signaling the time was bad. A white female medical worker touched me on the shoulder interrupting my conversation with the crack heads.

"Sir, I was told you were Valerie Bank's brother. We need you to ride over with her so we can get more information on her," the female medical worker stated. I had to say "yes" when I noticed the black detective was walking toward me.

He approached me with a serious stare on his face in which his facial expression had made me feel like he was looking through my soul. I didn't have time to be interrogated. That was why I agreed to ride with Val over to the hospital in the ambulance.

"Excuse me sir. My name is Officer Richard Bailey. I need to speak to you about this incident that just took place."

"Well, I'm on my way to the hospital with my sister."

"So, Valerie Banks is your sister?"

"Yes."

"So, what is your name?"

This Detective was putting pressure on me by the second. He hit me with two quick questions. I didn't want to say the wrong thing, so I said "I want to go to the hospital with Val."

"Do you mind riding with me?" The officer asked.

"I'd rather ride with my sister." I said.

I noticed a set of unmarked cars pulling up on the scene as I had entered the back of the ambulance. Something told me a dog was in one of those cars and my inner thought was right. A big German Sheppard exited the back of one of the cars as the ambulance pulled off. I knew this wouldn't be the last time I would come in contact with Detective Richard Bailey. Shit, I was selling dope in his district and my money was starting to show. My guess, it would be sooner than I thought.

CHAPTER 3

RHONDA

Place: The hospital 2 days later

I couldn't believe I had ridden in the ambulance with Jay because I didn't even know this guy. It was a scene like out of a gangster movie how we had met. Him getting shot in the leg and some of the buck shots reaching his right eye ball, in addition, the police asking me questions. I had refused to talk, but I stayed at the hospital to show my support for Jay.

Jay had to have a major operation on his right eye. The end result was he had a 50-50 chance the eye would regain sight. I felt like someone hit me in the gut with a base-ball bat, when I had heard this news. Even though I didn't know Jay as a person, yet, I felt like it was my fault he had gotten shot. If I hadn't been walking to the store that day, Jay wouldn't have been putting all his attention on me and he would have been on point when the three thugs had pulled in the neighborhood.

Jay's operation took several hours and after the operation his doctor had decided to keep him for a couple weeks. I stayed the first night and I laid in the bed next to him when the nurse had left out for the night. I decided to help Jay find the guys that had shot him. So, I decided to meet with the investigator on his case. I was in the hospital lobby waiting on the investigator to come talk to me, when the hospital medical workers had come through the sliding doors rolling a bed with a middle age black woman on the bed. She was hooked to a oxygen mask. Her clothes were bloody. A young man about my age, was walking right beside the lady's' bed, before he was asked by one of the medical workers to stay in the lobby. The young man took a seat across from me.

He was tall, slim built, brown skin, and had nice looking brown eyes. The seriousness in his eyes told me the woman they had rolled by me was an important person to him. This was what I was looking for in a man. Serious focus.

"Hello, is everything alright?" I asked

"Do I know you?" This guy responded.

"No, I was just trying to make conversation."

"Well, I'm not looking for a conversation."

"Excuse me," I responded "Sorry bad timing"

"No, I'm sorry."

It was something about his demeanor and his attitude that made me want to get to know him. A few minutes later, he asked, "What's your name?"

"My name is Rhonda"

"How long have you been waiting?"

"Now you want to talk to me."

"Look, I'm sorry about my attitude. My friend just got shot."

"I'm sorry to hear that."

"Why are you here?"

"One question at a time."

"First question. I've been here for two days. The answer to your second question is. I'm here for a friend too."

"Your boyfriend?'

"No. Just a guy I met."

"What happened to him?"

"He was shot."

"Damn! Is he alright?"

"He's going to make it, but he might have a little trouble seeing out of his right eye."

"I hope he will be alright."

"Me too."

"Can I buy you something out of the snack machine?"

"Do I look like I'm hungry?"

"Yes."

"You haven't even told me your name."

"Oh, I'm sorry. My name is Martez."

"Nice to meet you Martez." I wasn't used to playing the nice girl role, but I wanted to impress this guy.

"What side of town you from?" He asked.

"I'm from West Wood apartments. Between Wilkerson Blvd and Freedom Drive."

"I know the neighborhood."

"You do?" I asked.

This guy had my full attention now. He was really paying attention to everything that came out my mouth. He had also made eye-contact during our conversation, something I had learned to do from my counselor at Taps; A school I had to attended after I got pregnant by Dewayne.

"Now tell me where you are from?" I asked.

"I'm from the West side."

"What neighborhood?" I asked

Martez hesitated and said, "I grew up in Dalton Village Projects."

"That a crazy Place."

"How do you know?"

"I watch the news."

"The news tells lies."

"Plus the streets talk."

"Look, You right, my neighborhood is F'd up."

Martez said as he put his hand over his mouth.

Then he said, "I'm sorry for expressing myself with foul

words, but that's the true fact of the matter."

"My neighborhood is messed up too." I said as I crossed my arms across my chest. Then I continued, "Ever since the person that invented crack cocaine put this product out, it's been pure hell in my hood."

"The same stuff happened to my hood. Before the crack, it was safe. Now there are shoot-outs and all kinds of stuff going on in my hood."

"Look Martez," I said. Martez made direct eye-contact with me before I continued, "You might want to leave here before the investigator gets here. The TV screen in the lobby was showing the crime scene where Jay had been shot at. Martez hadn't seen my neighborhood on TV, or heard about the shooting, but then again Martez didn't seem like the type to watch the news. His appearance told a story of its own. The Timberland boots, baggy pants gave me the sign Martez was a dope-boy. Most of the guys in the city were rocking braids and the dread-locks, but Martez was sticking to the old fashioned 360 waves. He had the thick kind that looked like the kind a surfer would ride in the sun set in. Plus, his swagger was off the charts.

"So, you 5-0?"

"Hell No!" I shouted. Causing a semi-scene.

"Well, why are you meeting with the police?"

"Like I told you, I was with this guy that got shot. We were walking to the store when some guys pulled up and started shooting!". I responded.

"What are you planning to discuss with the police?"

"You sound like the police with all these questions!!"

A few seconds passed by before Martez spoke. "Look, it was nice to have met you, but I have to go."

"What about your friend?" I asked in a concerned tone.

"She will be alright." He responded quickly.

"How can I get in touch with you?"

"You sure you want to get involved with me?"

"I just want to be your friend."

"Why you can't give me your home number?"

"You sure you not 5-0?"

"No!"

"Just take this number and call me later. I want you to help keep a tab on my friend while you here." Martez said. Then he placed the number that he had written on a small piece of paper and reached it to me. I took the number and put it in my jean shorts pocket and looked back up at him. He was standing directly in front of me now. I took the pen that Martez had taken from the front desk and wrote down my best friend's home phone number. Then I gave it to him. He gave me a smile and turned and walked out the front entrance of the hospital. A few minutes later, a black, tall, slim-built man dressed in slacks, white cotton shirt, and black loafers walked through the front entrance of the hospital with a brief case in his hand. I watched as he stopped at the front medical check-in station and picked up a visitor pass. I knew this was investigator Richard Bailey from his demeanor. He talked with confidence to the check-in station. I had a conversation with investigator Mr. Bailey on the phone, the first day at the hospital, but due to another shooting incident that day, he did not come over to the hospital and interview me about Jay's incident. I really didn't want to get involved due to the fact I did not have anyone to protect me, or my baby from these guys that had shot Jay.

"How are you today Miss Norris?" Investigator Bailey asked as he extended his hand. I received his greeting with a smile.

"You must be investigator Bailey?"

"Yes, I am." Over my phone conversation with investigator Bailey I had given him a description of what I was wearing and where I was in the lobby. My mind was now running at a million miles a second. I did not want to say the wrong thing so when Investigator Bailey started drilling me about the shooting incident, I took a couple deep breaths and said, "I don't have information that can help your case."

"You told me on the phone two days ago that you could help me." He had responded quickly.

"I can't remember now."

"Did someone threaten you?"

"No."

"Well, why all of the sudden you can't remember the incident?"

"I don't want to get involved." I responded quickly.

"You were there so that makes you a witness."

"Like I said, I don't have information."

I could see that Investigator Bailey was not up to a cat and mouse game by his police behavior. He was really interested in finding out who shot Jay. Investigator Bailey had drilled me with some more questions before he decided to conclude the interview. "Here is my card. If you decide you want to help your boyfriend, then you call me." Investigator Bailey had said as he gave me his card. I took the card and put it in my pocket.

"If anything comes to mind, I will call you." I said then turned to walk away. Investigator Bailey touched my shoulder after I turned towards the front entrance and said, "What if that was you laying up in that hospital bed? Do you think Jay would help?" I turned back towards him.

The question had caught me totally off guard. I really did not have a answer for this investigator. So I said "I don't have anything for you Detective Bailey." I turned and headed towards the front entrance of the gift shop. It surprised me that Detective Bailey did not follow me being that he was persistent at his on-going investigation. I entered the small B-shaped room that was called the hospital gift shop. It was filled with all kinds of get well-cards and teddy bears. I was at the shop for a gift, and to talk to Jay's sister. I had met with her the day Jay was shot. She still had her hair under her uniform matching cap like the day Jay was shot. She was a shade darker than Jay, and she had the same hair color and height as her brother. If I didn't know better, I would have thought they were twins. She had let it be known that she was Jays big sister and she cared a lot about him. I had explained to Vanessa that I was present when Jay was shot and I did not know who the shooter was, but she did not believe me. Vanessa had already pre-judged me as being a young gold-digger. She rolled her eyes as I picked up a card off the counter and placed it in front of her to ring-up. She grabbed the card and put it in a bag. Then tossed it to me. "I don't know what's wrong with you?"

"You got my brother shot." She said.

"No, I did not!"

"Word on the street is you got him shot because you messing around with some gang members from outer-state!"

"Well, you got the story all wrong." I said back in a ghetto attitude. "If I find out you got my brother shot, you going to have problems!"

CHAPTER 4

MARTEZ

I wasn't in the mood to make a love connection with Rhonda due to the fact Val had been shot, but I still gave her my number. Rhonda was new to being in a situation like the one she was in. I could tell this by the conversation we had had in the lobby of the hospital. I was looking forward to getting in her panties, since she had told me she did not have a boyfriend. I felt weird over the next few days, because I couldn't stop thinking about Rhonda.

The sound of my cousin Telly's voice interrupted my dream about Rhonda when he knocked on the door at my new dope spot.

"Martez, open up the door." My cousin shouted.

"I'm coming. I'm coming!" I shouted as I put my shirt on and slipped on my Nikes. I could hear the rain pouring down. My cousin was standing at the door along with my best friend Melvin. They both were dressed in blue new warm-up suits and matching Nike shoes. Standing well over 6 foot tall in height, both of these guys looked like NBA basketball players. Both of them had brown paper bags in their hands. I could tell by the neck of the bottles that it was alcohol.

"What are you two doing here this early in the morning?" I asked as I opened the door with one hand and wiped one of my eyes with the other one.

"Man, we heard about what happened at your old dope spot. So we came here to see if you are doing okay." My cousin said after he and my best-friend had stepped through the door.

I decided to change location because Detective Bailey was still trying to get me to help make a case against the guys in the black Cadillac. I had found a spot on the opposite end of my grandmothers' neighborhood since all my clientele was from her hood.

"How did you two find out about this spot?"

"You know the word spread through the streets like a wild fire. Plus, your mother told my mother you moved in across the street from your grandmother's." My cousin responded.

This spot was totally different from Val's house because I was now in the heart of Dalton Village Projects. In addition, this was one of the most crime infested projects in the city of Charlotte. The buildings of Dalton Village Projects were made up of brown-sand color red bricks and stood two stories high with solid wooden doors. The neighborhood had over five thousand people staying together in it, which then looked like a pack of roaches when everyone was outside.

"What are you two up too." I asked.

"We were thinking about hitting the gym." Melvin responded quickly. Then my cousin said. "We got some suckers wanting to gamble against us. They want to put up a couple hundred on a three-on-three match."

"I told you two, I ain't with that bull-shit no more. It's too much money in the drug game to be out bouncing a basketball," I said.

"These are some suckers from my job," My cousin responded.

My cousin had always been the type of guy to look for easy

prey to take money from ever since he had decided to drop out of college a few months in his first semester. Now Melvin on the other hand was totally different from Telly and myself. He looked forward to being the first person with the latest fashion and that was why he had turned to selling drugs after his mother went to federal prison for a drug charge. Before his mother went off to prison, she was providing all of Melvin's needs and wants with the drug money. By losing his mother to the federal prison system, it was like I lost my childhood friend Melvin, to the drugs and alcohol, because he had begun using to hide the real pain of his mother being in prison.

A knock at the back door interrupted our conversation.

"See what I'm saying. I have biz to conduct while y'all play ball." I said.

My cousin smiled while Melvin let out a small laugh at my humorous comment. Then I headed to the back door in the kitchen area after leaving the small living room. This junkie by the name of Fast Eddie was standing outside the door with his back pack on his back when I peeked out of the door.

"Whats up Eddie?" I asked.

"I need a eight ball!" He responded. He was dressed in jeans, T-shirt and old Nikes.

You know I don't like selling weight. I got some rocks" I said.

Eddie was a stone-cold crack head, but he was also a hustler at heart. His main hustle was cutting hair in the neighborhood. He could cut anything in side your head if you had hair. I had been the first kid in my hood to have the Jordan symbol cut inside my hair by Fast Eddie.

"Man, I need a eight ball so I can get with this white chick around the corner" Eddie lied.

"Take these ten rocks and put them together and you will have a eight ball" I said as I pulled out a bag full of twenty rocks.

I was surprised Eddie did not protest and I was also thrilled that Eddie had the right amount of money because he was always coming two or three dollars short. I put the money inside my pocket as I watched Eddie walk towards a black Cadillac. This car looked similar to the vehicle that was at the scene the day Val was shot. My mind told me this was the car. Panic filled my body as I reached for the .45 hand gun and learned that it was not under the refrigerator. I had circled my hand around the rim of the bottom of the machine in search of the gun. I realized it was not in the spot I had placed it in. Empty. Zero. Nothing. This small box shaped kitchen did not have too many places I could hide a gun. The kitchen cabinets and shelves were empty. There was only a table and three wooden chair stationed inside the room. I closed the back door quickly and I headed back to the common area of my crack spot. My cousin and my best friend had made themselves at home by kicking off their shoes and firing up a blunt of weed. Telly or Melvin did not say a word as I rushed through the room like a mad man and headed up the stairs in a sprint. Once upstairs, I walked in the master bedroom and opened the closet. Then I searched the closet for my gun. My play sister, Lorna, was always getting on me about hiding my gun where her son could find it so she was always moving my gun if she found it in a spot where her son could get to it. The last time I had put it in a spot where her son could find it, she had scolded me before she told me it was inside her bedroom closet inside the pocket of her leather jacket.

Once again, the gun was inside the leather jacket. I had tossed all the clothes inside the drawers on the bed. When I had finished the search of the large drawer inside the small box shaped bedroom, I rushed over to the night stand. Inside the night stand was my hollow point bullets in a small brown paper bag. I grabbed the bullets and loaded up my pistol. Then I headed quickly back down stairs. Telly was dumping ashes inside the glass ash tray when I walked though the room with the gun in my hand. Melvin's eyes lit up like a deer standing in front of headlights. He knew something was wrong due to the pistol in my hand. I had not told my cousin or my best friend the full details of how Val was shot out front of her house, or how I was faced with this Black Cadillac at my new crack spot. This car was the same car that was used when Val was shot. The tint on the windows made me come to this conclusion. My best friend walked in the kitchen while I was looking out the window. I turned in his direction for a second before I turned my attention back to the black Cadillac in the back parking lot of the building. Eddie was now talking to the driver of the car while showing him the rocks he had purchased from me. Something told me Eddie had lied, but I had still served him.

"What's up Martez?" Melvin asked me.

"This car looks like the same car that was at Val's spot when she was shot."

Melvin moved in closer and took a look out at the black Cadillac, Eddie was now bending over in. Melvin let the curtain go after recognizing the car from the kitchen window.

"I know that car," Melvin said with panic in his voice.

"Who are those guys?"

"They are gang members from the West Coast. They just got down to this city about a month ago."

"How do you know them?"

"They are gang members."

"What do you mean gang members?"

"They are Bloods!"

"What the hell is Bloods?" I had never known there were serious gangs around the world. The only gangs I knew about were gangs like the G-men, He-men, and the neighborhood drug gangs in Charlotte.

"That car is the car that was involved in the shooting at Val's house. I did not see who shot her, but I am sure that's the car." I stated.

Melvin stepped back from me and stared deep in to my eyes and said, "You don't want to mess with them. Those guys are real-killers!"

"How do you know?" I asked with concern in my voice.

"Just look at the body count since last month. There has been five murders and a dozen assaults around the city since they arrived!"

"How do you know so much about them?"

"Just say, I met the head man in charge. He is the O-G!"

"What is a O-G?"

"You've got a lot to learn. Look, Martez, I think it's best you get down with these guys."

"Hell no! Ain't no one going to take my spot!"

"They already took your spot you had at Val's!"

"What are you talking about?"

"They moved in. They got Val's house off the hook!"

"I had left Val's house because the police! They got the spot what the hell are you talking about? Who told you this!?"

"Word on the streets is they are planning to take West Blvd."

"I have not heard this word until now. I do not know anything about a gang or anyone taking over West Blvd."

This information was all new to me and I did not know how I could use this information until Melvin spoke. "There are some other gang members from the West Coast that don't like the Bloods."

"Who are these guys?"

"They are the Crips. Their colors are blue."

"How do you know about them?"

"I saw a couple of them put in work at club Bee-Bee. They shot up a crowd of people and dropped a flag on the ground at the scene."

"What is a flag?" I asked.

"It's a bandana. Red is for the Bloods and Blue is for the Crip." Melvin said.

The black Cadillac pulled out the parking lot after the driver reached Eddie some dope. The exchange did not seem like there was a problem, but I could not stop thinking about how slow the Cadillac had pulled out of the parking lot. It was like the guys in the car were making notes of the surrounding area because the passenger had let down the window and looked at the numbers on my dope spot.

RHONDA

It didn't take long for Jay and I to become a couple. His sister didn't like this idea because of the robbery incident, but Jay convinced her that it was not my fault he had gotten shot and that he was in love with me. He didn't care that I had a kid. My daughter and I had moved in with Jay and his sister after I found out Jay was 80% blind in his right eye. It was like the beginning of my closure when I had decided to move in with Jay and his sister because I felt guilty about Jay getting shot. When I had arrived with my daughter on Camp Green Road in a cab, I thought I would get a warm welcome, but to my surprise, Jay was at a doctor's appointment and his sister was the only person at home. She was dressed in tight jeans, tank top, and boots. Her fake hair was hanging down close to her cheeks. She let me know that she was the queen of the castle and I was a visitor in her eyes. I really didn't want any drama with Jay's sister due to the fact that she was his only sister and she had been taken care of Jay since their mother had died when Jay was only three. Vanessa was 16 years older than Jay and she did not look a day older than 30. Even though she was in her late 30's, she had it going on. After putting away all my stuff and putting my daughter in Jay's bed, I re-entered the common area of the three-bedroom house. Vanessa was now sitting on the soft white leather couch painting her nails. She glanced up at me then continued her personal manicure. I took a seat across from her on the love seat and said "Can you cook?"

"What kind of question is that?" Vanessa asked.

"I was just asking because I can."

"Well, that's my kitchen and I don't want you up in it messing around!"

"Jay told me you like to go out a lot to eat so that's why I asked you if you could cook!"

"I'm confused about why he moved you and your baby in."

"I don't want to fight against you Vanessa. I really just want to be your friend for Jay's sake."

"Well, I am not looking for a friend. I don't know what my brother told you, but I don't hang out with kids that have kids!"

"I am not a kid!" I said in protest.

"Jay told me your age. The only reason I am going along with you and his relationship is I think he really likes you. I've never seen my brothers' eyes light up like they do when you are around."

"Look, I am not here to come in between ya'll relationship. He told me how close ya'll are and I respect that."

"I appreciate your respect for my brother and my relationship with him, but that still ain't going to make me like you. I want you to know I grew up in the hood too and I recognize game when I see it."

"What are you talking about?" I asked.

"I know you after my brother's money!" She said.

"What money?"

"Please girlfriend, don't act like you don't know!"

Vanessa had said and stressed every single word in her ghetto attitude. I really didn't know what Vanessa was talking about when she said I was after Jay's money. Jay hadn't discussed with me about a stash or anything of that nature. The only money I knew about was the couple thousand Jay had passed off to me when the three guys in the Cadillac had pulled up on him and shot him the day we met.

"Jay has not told me about anything about any money." I said back to Vanessa in a stern serious voice.

"Please Rhonda, save the games for a TV show."

"I'm for real Vanessa. I really don't know what you are talking about."

"So, Jay didn't tell you about his money?"

"No!" I responded.

Vanessa dropped the nail brush back into the small bottle after she asked me if Jay had told me about his money. Then she pulled her long hair into a pony tail, wrapped a rubber band around it then continued. "So, you don't know about the money Jay received when he turned 21."

"No, I do not!"

Vanessa stared at me for a moment. It was like she was trying to read me like a book. I knew she knew I didn't know about the money Jay had received when he turned 21.

"So Jay didn't tell you the story about our mother?"

"He told me your mother died from cancer and that was it."

"He did not tell you about the life insurance money my mother left him?"

"No."

This was new information that Jay didn't inform me about before I had decided to move in with him and Vanessa. This was really a shock to me that Jay had more money than I thought he had because I really did not think he had much money since he was in West Wood Apartments selling crack rocks. I knew Jay wasn't a baller. "I just don't believe you Rhonda. I think you are after my brothers' dead presidents."

"You got me tagged all wrong. I don't want your brother's money. I really like Jay. We have been through a lot in a short amount of time."

"You sound like you trying to get a role on the day-time soaps. I just don't trust you."

"You don't know me, Vanessa."

The house phone interrupted our conversation. Vanessa grabbed the phone and turned in the opposite direction and started a conversation with the caller. I walked back to Jay's room and did a little rearranging before Jay arrived an hour later from the eye-doctor. He came walking in like the rapper SLICK RICK with a black eye patch over his right eye, minus the big gold chains.

"You need help?" I asked.

"No" He responded

"Ok."

"Where is my sister?" He asked.

I hesitated after grabbing my blue jean Daisy Duke shorts off the dresser and said "She left after she got off the phone."

"How long ago?"

"About 30 minutes ago."

Jay struggled over to the small closet and opened the door. Then he grabbed a shoe box off the top shelf and put a stack of bills in the box. I walked back to the living room. I did not take this all-black middle-class neighborhood as being a crime infested place, but this neighborhood was surrounded by Columbus Circle and my mother's neighborhood Westwood apartments in which both of these hoods were low-income and drug infested. So, when Jay pulled out a black 9 millimeter, I knew this was his weapon to protect his money and drugs. I did not want to be a pest to Jay so I asked him "What's my position on your team?"

He stated "My girlfriend/house mate"

I did not protest the role as house mate because I knew he was adding me to his team to watch his drugs and money while he ran the streets. Jay had shown me how the gun worked by displaying a small class between him and me in the backyard. I had taken the gun inside my hand after Jay had shown me how to hold the gun in front of me. The sixteen shot black clip had already been inserted by Jay seconds before he had given me the weapon.

"Now Rhonda, I want you to point in the air and pull the trigger." Jay had said. "No Jay!"

"Why?"

"My daughter is asleep!"

"She won't hear it. I promise."

"NO JAY!"

"No one is going to know that we are over here having target practice with the air. Just point the gun in the air and pull the trigger."

"I don't want to wake up my daughter!"

"You ain't. Trust me?"

I had decided to pull the trigger after looking over the skyline for a few seconds. The flame from the gun had scared me because it lit up close to my face. "Holy Shit!" I had shouted as I felt the jerk of the gun.

"Are you ok?" Jay had asked.

"Yes." I said.

I had felt like I had overcome my fear in a blink of an eye because after I had fired the pistol. It was like the fear had left my body. My nerves were all off track at first and my arm pits and hands were sweating. Plus, I could smell gun powder at that time. But I was okay.

"Take this gun." I had said.

"You sure you all right?" Jay asked. He was laughing now.

"Yes." I responded.

The sound of a police siren had been heard off in the cool night atmosphere. This had sent Jay running toward the back door.

"What's wrong Jay?" I had asked.

"Someone probably called the police." He had stated.

"I thought it was safe to shoot in the air."

"I just wanted to teach you how to shoot."

"Why?" I had asked.

"Come in the house and I will explain."

Several minutes later Jay came walking out his bedroom after he had checked on my daughter. Now he had a bag in his hand. I took a seat on the couch where Vanessa had been doing her in-home manicure earlier. Jay walked over to the glass table that sat in the middle of the room and pulled out a baseball size white looking rock.

"Do you know what this is?" Jay asked.

I had seen crack inside vials but not in a full baseball size like Jay was holding in his hand. This was all new since I had never really thought about messing around with a drug dealer. The only guys I had dealt with in the past were guys I went to Junior high school with and older men I had sex with just for money. This was a whole new world to me, because Jay was not like one of the young men I had sex with for fun or like the old men that paid me for a quick nut. He really wanted me to be his partner in crime and not just a sex object like all the other guys.

"No." I lied.

I did not want to run Jay off by saying I knew it was crack because my sixth sense told me if I revealed too much to him that he would dismiss me like a class. "I want you to know this is crack. This is how I make my money." Jay said as he pulled a new set of razors out the black bag. Then he continued his speech.

"The number one rule to the ten rules of selling crack is [don't get high on your own supply.]"

I knew the first two-rules from the small-time dealers inside my mother's neighborhood. They were always stressing the sayings to most of the fiends that walked up asking for credit. "Rule number two. Never give a crack head credit. You think he's going to pay you back, FORGET IT!"

These rules were rolling off Jay's tongue like they had been instilled in him by someone that was more advanced in years as far as the drug game. When Jay got to rule number three, instantly I thought about the episode at the hospital with Martez. He had already prepared me about how to deal with the cops. Now rule number four. Never trust nobody. This was a serious rule to me because being violated at the age of 12 by my mother's boyfriend made me not trust people. "Rule number five. Move in silence." Jay stated. I had to ask Jay what the meaning of moving in silence was in the crack game. He stated, "You can't be flashy. If I give you money to buy nice things. I don't want you to be too flamboyant."

"I'm confused about this rule. Why, have money and not spend it?"

"That a good question. That why I'm going to answer it for you." Jay said.

Jay pulled out a black small digital scale and placed it on the table beside the baseball sized crack rock. Then he said. "People want to be in my position. They will rob, steal, and kill for this stuff." Then he pointed at the crack cocaine. I already knew this, but I was still dumbfounded to the fact that people robbed people just out of hate. Jay exposed this fact to me when he said. "You have haters and you have people that get hated on. There is no in between." Jay had a nice concept about how people perceived each other in life. My concept was totally different since I had grown up without money. Jay continued "Rule number six. Never sell crack where you rest your head at. I don't care if they want a ounce. Tell them to bounce."

After Jay went through rule seven, eight, nine, and ten, I felt like I had just graduated from Jay's school of street crack game! This was truly a new element I was tapping into because Jay thought I was just young, dumb, and full of cum. I knew I had to play my position to stay out of the ghetto. It was going to be nice to sleep in a king-sized bed with a real man with money instead of sleeping in a bunk bed that was almost two sizes too small for my body. My life was now in a new direction. It was far from wearing and sharing the same pair of jeans with my sisters. When Jay came to bed the first night with me, I decided right then that I would do just what he wanted me to do. I served Jay like a waitress at a fancy restaurant. He ate out my ass like he was eating at all you can eat buffet. I returned the favor because I was trying to lock up my position on Jay's little team. He did not pay attention to me at all after the sex act, but his money made me feel like I was moving on up like the Jefferson's. Something was still missing from my life because I felt empty as I laid next to Jay after he had fallen asleep.

CHAPTER 5

MARTEZ

Icouldn't stop thinking about the black Cadillac that had pulled up in the back parking lot of my new dope spot. My sixth sense was telling me that these guys were the same guys that had shot Val. Melvin had given me enough information to start my own investigation on these guys. In which he had told me that these guys had a pool hall off the corner of Remount Rd. I knew the spot, because I used to go to a night club, right across the street from the pool hall. Melvin also had told me they had set up a dope spot in the back of this neighborhood called "Sand Hurst apartments." These apartments were made up of middle low class black families that lived in these apartments before the new owner. Once the new owner took over this neighborhood it became totally drug infested. It became the perfect location for the West Coast MOB Gang, to sell drugs in.

These guys had been taking turf on West Blvd at a rapid pace and they were also recruiting new members to join their gang. The only qualifications that new members needed to join their gang was street credibility and access to a gun. This drug gang stuff was not new to me but the West coast MOB gang members had a different type outlook when it came to being a gang member. They carried around with them a red bandana and call it their flag. In addition, they all like to wear red to represent their gang. I arrived at the pool hall after I had paid a junkie a twenty rock to borrow his car. It did not take me long to find out who was the Omega male out of the five-foot soldiers that were standing outside the building. This guy had on a red t-shirt, jean, and a black fitted cap. I made eye contact with this guy once I put the car in park. It was my duty to not be intimidated by these thugs since they looked for weakness in their prey.

"State your biz." The Omega male said.

"I'm here to shoot pool." I responded.

"We are closed right now."

I turned to walk back to the rental car when I noticed a bald head big 300-pound dude in a red dress suit stepping out a black van. He glanced over at me as he made his way to the pool hall entrance.

"Make way for the OG." One of the sidekicks said as this big guy walked through the group of young thugs so he could enter the pool hall. I knew this was the OG that Melvin had told me about. I did not know how I was going to get close to him, but I knew I would have to get close to him to find out his plans. Melvin's words had echoed in the back of my mind.

"You need to get down with the Bloods."

My streets instincts kicked in. I had to get this guy's attention. So, I shouted. "Are you the OG?"

"Who's asking?" the big guy asked.

"I'm a friend of Melvin's. He told me you wanted to see me?" The OG made a face like he was searching for Melvin's face. "Who you?"

"I'm Martez."

"Martez who?"

"Martez from Farmer St."

The OG looked me dead in the eyes. I knew what he was trying to do. His intimidation stare did not work on me like it did to his members. "So, Melvin told you about me?" He asked.

"Yes, that's why I'm here."

"So you want to get put down?"

This question caught me off guard. I did not come to the Bloods to enter their way of life. I just wanted to let them know I knew they were in the city and I did not agree with the way they were operating around the city.

"I'm not here to get put down. I'm here to let you know that I run Farmer Street. That's my spot."

"I can tell you was not here to put in work for my cause. So, therefore, you need to leave before one of my soldiers have to gain some rank!" I did not want to make this guy mad, but I had to make a stand.

"I don't want no trouble, but remember Farmer Street is my turf."

"I got to give it to you, lil' bro, you got heart. That's why I'm going to let you stay alive."

I knew I had over stepped my boundary when I told this OG, Farmer St. was mine. I could tell from the sound of his response that my life would be in danger after this meeting. When I returned to my dope spot, where Melvin was waiting, I knew the OG had been in contact with Melvin. He was nervous and shaking like a fiend that was trying to kick the habit.

"What did you say to the OG?" Melvin asked.

"I told him Farmer St. is mine."

"Why did you do that?"

"You know the saying. If you don't stand for something, you will fall for anything."

"Right now isn't the time to be standing up for a dope spot. Your life is more important."

"Look Melvin, I ain't afraid of those Bloods. My veins pump

Blood not Kool-aid."

"You can't play with these guys. They are real killers. They kill for fun!"

"Remember we all bleed the same. Blood is blue until it leaves the body and hits the air."

"I love you like a brother. I don't want to have to come to your funeral," Melvin said then took off towards the waiting car that was parked right in front of the parking lot where my grandmother's building was located. Melvin pointed at my grandmother's building as he crossed the street. I knew he was pointing out the weakness in my chain. My grandmother living in the projects was a weak link in my chain, but that was not going to stand in my way of building me an empire. I walked inside my dope spot to find my play sister sitting on the couch with tears in her eyes. I knew something was very wrong. This was the first time I had seen my play sister in tears.

"What's wrong sis?" I asked.

She looked up at me. Then she put her head back between her lap after covering her face. I did not want to push my sister farther into her distress so I made my way into the kitchen. Once inside the kitchen, I noticed why she was crying. In a big bold word that was painted in cat blood was the word "Blood." Instantly, I knew who put this stint together, but I did not know who could get inside the apartment with someone not seeing who it was. My sister did not feel good being inside the apartment due to the dead cat's smell. I did not object when she said she was going to stay with her mother for a while. I cleaned up the apartment and then I called my connect Ty on his shop phone. "Gold rims & trims."

"We need to talk." I said.

"You ready for some new tires?" He asked.

"I'm ready."

"Same type from last time."

"Yes, but I need to talk to you about some other stuff."

"Half an hour. Meet me at my brother's shop on the Plaza Rd."

Tyron had hung up before I could get another word out my mouth. He did not like to talk business on the phone, especially drug business. Ty pulled up in his 400LS Lexus. He was the only black young guy I knew who had a shop to cover up his drug business. Plus, he had his sister doing business for him to clean up the drug money he was making on the streets of Charlotte. Ty was what you call a Heavy Hitter. He was moving kilos by the boat load. His crew consisted of his two brothers Mark and Curtis. They were his underclassmen in which they could put together gun crews if trouble ever came knocking. At this point, trouble was knocking and knocking hard. I knew I could count on Ty for help because I was moving tons of cocaine for him. Even though I was buying most of my product from him, he had always told me if I ran into any trouble that I could not handle then give him a call. I was sitting in the lobby of the tire shop reading an Ebony magazine when Ty walked in. He was dressed in black slacks, white dress shirt, and black gator shoes. Standing at six foot even, he was three inches shorter than me and thin and skinny like a tooth pick.

"Martez, step to the side of the building." Ty said as he pointed to the outside.

I knew he was being cautious because talking inside the tire shop about street business was a risk and the fact he had once found a wiretap inside it didn't make it any better. Ty told me about the wiretap right after it had happened. The sun was going down and light wind was blowing trash from the restaurant beside Ty's brother's shop. Ty picked up trash while I followed him to the side of the building. A large package was sitting on the back patio when we had reached the back of the shop. Ty gave me the package and said "I can see something is really wrong with you. It's written all over your face."

I took the package and said, "I ran into some new breed of

hustlers."

"Do you have a problem?" Ty asked.

I knew Ty had connections with bondsmen, lawyers, and some of the top business owners around the city. He was young at age, but wise beyond his years. This is what I liked most about him. His wisdom was something I wish I had. When it came to handling situations in the streets, I had heard about the small wars he had won with his crew when it came to handling situations in the streets. In the streets of Charlotte, a name carried weight when it came to being a Heavy Hitter into the city. Ty was a major heavy hitter due to the fact he had two killers known to the streets as Gemini and Taurus. He only let them loose when his brothers Mark and Curtis could not stop the bleeding of other crews that wanted their spot. I decided to be truthful with Ty, because I did not want to start a war that I could not participate in. I was truthfully a hustler at heart and guns were not something I specialized in. Truthfully, I knew how to shoot, but I want to be a street Millionaire.

"I need help with these new Blood Gang members. They have moved in on my space."

"I heard about the incident that happened at Val's house. Why didn't you tell me about that?"

"I did not want you to get involved. I thought I could let that blow over, but I found out the Bloods shot Val and they were selling out her house."

"The word on the streets is you tucked your tail and ran."

"I just relocated due to the cops."

"Look Martez, I know you are a hustler. Guns are for killers. You have to choose between selling crack cocaine or being a gunman."

"That's what I want to talk to you about. I have been thinking about making me enough money and then exit the game."

"You sound like I used to. When I was your age, I was standing out on the corner on Hemphill Street selling drugs to anyone who would purchase them."

"I don't want to sell dope all my life. I want to get a couple of businesses like you and get out."

"You think these businesses are making the type of money to live this life style?" Ty said as he pointed to himself.

I listened closely as he continued. "I paid my dues in the streets. I built my clientele up so I could live like I want to. I be damn if these Bloods going to take my spot."

Ty knew the rules to the game. If his team showed any sign of weakness, he would earn a target on his back. At the moment, we had a target on our backs. I paid Ty his money before I put the package of cocaine in the trunk of my car. Then I said. "Send the best. Don't play with these dudes."

"They are marked men due to all the red they wear." Ty said before he cracked a smile exposing his mouth full of pinkish reddish diamonds in his gold teeth.

I knew I had started a war, but I did not know how serious the war would get or last. I went back to my dope spot to find out that the first body of this war was found on the corner of West Blvd and Remount Rd. a block from the pool hall. Ty had sent Taurus over to the pool hall to put in some work. Taurus had taken a bullet to the head and chest. The funeral was sad. Closed Casket.

RHONDA

2 months later…

I could not believe I was on my way to Martez's dope spot. It did not take me long to decide to make the trip across town after Jay had taken his pain medication and fell into a deep sleep. My V-spot was boiling over like some hot water in a pot from the phone sex I had had with Martez earlier. Just thinking about Martez's voice made me moist and horny. Jay was not providing the care to feed my tremendous appetite that my body was craving for in bed. Our sex life was now non-existent due to Jay always complaining about his wounds. I did not blame Jay for not providing the care of my sexual needs, and I really did not care much for his oral sex either, due to the fact he was a rookie. I had more experience in that area because I was taught at an early age when I had been molested by my mother's boyfriend. The leather seats in the cab felt hot against my skin. It was summer and the night was cool but my body temperature felt like two hundred. I did not know if it was the anticipation of having sex with Martez or just me being nervous and vulnerable due to Jay's neglect. My armpits and my palms were sweating even though the air conditioning was blowing on high inside the cab. The cab driver noticed me biting my nails and asked "Is everything alright?" I hesitated and said, "Everything is ok with me."

"I was just asking because the address you gave me on Farmer Street, on the West side is a drug infested area."

"I know."

"Are you on drugs?" He asked.

"Are you the damned police?"

"No." He responded quickly.

"Well, why da hell are you asking me questions!"

"I'm sorry. I just don't like to go in that area. Too much killing!"

I noticed the cab driver had gray hair after he had taken off his old beat-up hat. He looked old enough to be my grandfather.

"People get shot and killed everywhere in this city." I stated.

"Not like on West side. West Blvd. is a known drug infested area."

"Tell me something new."

"You know we have to go there to get to Farmer St. The junkies over there are all over the place. They will try to rob you quicker than God will get the news.

"Just get me there, old man!"

"I hope you got my money. I don't need you jumping out my cab. I have grandkids I have to feed."

I did not say another word to the cab driver for the rest of the ride. The little conversation we had was cut short because I did not want to be reminded that I was headed to a war zone. I asked the cab driver for his cab number after I paid him a ten-dollar bill from the stack of money Jay had given me. He replied. "42." I took in the number and placed it inside my memory bank and headed toward the address Martez had given me. It was two am in the morning and I was out walking in a neighborhood looking for the black numbers on top of the front of the apartment like Martez had told me to look for. The neighborhood was made up of old red brick two story buildings with hard wooden doors. The buildings were built in the early 70's but they looked older. There were several light poles in the low-income neighborhood but most of the lights had been shot out, making the area dim lit. In my eyes, it was a perfect place to sell drugs due to the facts of the location and the missing lights. A rotten horse's smell hit my nose as I reached the address Martez had given me over the phone. This was my first time smelling the terrible smell that Martez had described to me over the phone. If I did not know the smell was caused by the rain entering the tainted soil, I would have thought a new dead animal was in the area.

Martez opened the front door as I stepped up on the porch. He was dressed in a long house coat and matching blue slippers. I could see his semi-built chest sticking out. The house coat in addition his brown skin was shining from some type of oil in his skin. I could smell lemon. I walked slowly into the apartment and realized Martez was living at this residence. The common room had a new floor mat, shaped sofa, two glass end tables, and a single black chair that matched the love seat beside the large wooden picture shelf. There was not a single picture on the shelf, but the shelf made the black leather furniture look in place. I fell in love with this three-bedroom apartment instantly. Martez's taste for nice things made Jays taste look like animal dung.

"Make yourself at home." Martez said.

I could tell in his voice he was just excited as me. "Do you tell all the women this when they come over?"

I was a little jealous at the moment. This might sound crazy, but I'm going to go out on a limb and say it anyway. My alter ego could not stop thinking about how many chicks had been laying around Martez's little crib playing house, butt-naked.

"I'm not going to tell you a lie. I have had a few women over a time, or two."

"O- You have?" I asked with an attitude.

"Before I met you."

"You don't have to pump my head up. I'm smart when it comes to men." I stated.

"I ain't trying to pump your head up. Right now I don't have a woman. I just have friends like you."

"What do you mean FRIENDS LIKE ME!?" I asked as if I had my ghetto attitude going on.

"I don't want to get myself in trouble so I'm going to stop talking." Martez said with a grin.

"That's what I want you to do."

"Not talk?" He asked as he looked me dead in my eyes. Instantly, we made a connection. I could feel my nipples growing by the seconds. Then my V-spot became so wet that I could have started a rain storm right there in Martez's common area. The way I answered Martez's question was by reaching out to him with my hands. He met my touch with his soft hands and we engulfed in a instant tongue wrestling match. We continued our lustful kiss while we made our way to the pillow soft love seat. I reached for Martez's dick as he had pulled down his boxer shorts. It was already rock hard. The large vein on the outer layer of his penis was sticking out like his penis was carrying a small back pack. When I made eye contact with Martez's love muscle, I knew he would be someone special in my life. The shape of his dick was different from most men. Most of the men I had been with was smaller in size and length. Jay was a mere eight inches, but small in width. Martez looked to be thick in width and 12 inches long.

I pulled off my Daisy-Duke shorts and my thong underwear while stroking Martez with my free hand. Then I helped guide his manhood inside my V-shape. "Ah... Ah..." I let out several moaning sounds while taking all 12 inches of Martez inside of me. He felt great with every thrust as he went deeper into my tunnel. I gripped him tight with my woman hood as we found a steady rhythm. "Oh Yes." He said. His words sounded like sweet music to my ears. I could tell Martez was enjoying my tunnel because he began to suck on my neck while he continued to pump in and out of me. "Don't!!" I shouted.

Martez hesitated for a second then he made eye contact with me and then asked. "Do you want me to stop?"

"No" I said in a whisper.

"Well, why did you say don't?" Martez asked while he continued to make sweet love to my womanhood. I could feel every inch of his dick because his huge vein was rubbing against my G-spot. "My spot! My spot! Damn my spot!"

"You know I have a relationship with Jay. It would be hard to explain a red mark on my neck." I stated in a whisper.

"Do you love him?" He asked.

"I think I do." I was breathing heave.

"Well, why are you here with me?"

"I don't know."

"Do you know I'm fucking you without a rubber?"

I could feel Martez's flesh hot against mine and semi droplets of sweat hitting my skin as he continued to pound inside of me. He felt so good inside of me, especially when he grabbed my shoulders and pulled me against his flesh to reach deeper. "Please Martez! Don't cum inside of me. You know I'm staying with Jay. How would I explain myself to him if I got pregnant by you?"

My statement only made Martez pump harder inside my pussy. It seemed to me like the statement turned him on. I wasn't trying to sound sexy or pillow talk with Martez about my life with Jay, but I really did not want to come up pregnant after going through what I went through with my first child by DeWayne. At the moment, I could not afford to have another kid or take care of another child due to my situation. I did not have support from my parents like most young teenage girls because my mother was addicted to alcohol and my father was addicted to crack cocaine and to top the whole situation off, I was staying with Jay. Martez began to breathe harder by the second. I could feel his manhood contracting like it was about to explode like a volcano. His eyes were closed tight and his mouth was back sucking my neck. I could not resist Martez any longer and I did not protest to his lustful affection toward my skin in which I really did not have a choice because he was holding me tight. When Martez began to bite my neck, this triggered the crazy freak in me that I never knew was a part of me. It was like my spirit transformed into another spirit from him biting me. In response, I started biting him back savagely. All of a sudden, I felt really wet between my legs. It felt like someone had thrown some warm water in between my legs. This feeling was totally different from the wet feelings that I had received at the hands of Jay when he gave me oral sex. My older sister Tanika had tried on several occasions to explain to me about a real orgasm, but I did not take the time to listen. I had been close to one on a few occasions with Jay but the moment of truth was finally at hand.

My body began to shake out of control like I was having a seizure. Then I felt the release of my hot juices being released. It was like my brain stood totally still as all the stress was then released from my body. I felt totally refreshed like I had just received a breath of fresh air after being under water on the verge of dying.

Before I could utter a word, Martez turned me over doggy style and re-entered his pole inside my love tunnel. He was still rock hard after the first round of our lustful love making. Even though he busted a nut too, his energy level was still extra high. I knew he was out to prove himself to me, because he was pulling me by my shoulders as he pounded away at my V-shape. I could not hold back any longer. Martez's heat from his body and his knife cutting sexual comments that he was shooting in my ear as he continued to please me sent me into another phase of lustful pleasure. Then I began to release my juices on his pole again! "Ah... Ah..." I said as I exhaled after releasing again. I knew this was the beginning of a crazy relationship due to the fact I had met Martez at the hospital while Jay was recovering from his gunshot wounds. Never in a thousand years would I imagine that sex with a man would be so mind blowing, but Martez made me change all my negative thoughts about sex after our first night together as one. It had been a while since I had some mind-blowing sex.

CHAPTER 6

MARTEZ

The next morning.

I couldn't stop thinking about Rhonda when she had left me lying in bed. She had really put her mark on me. Especially, when we climaxed at the same time. I knew her mother was staying in West Wood, but I did not know exactly where her mother's building was located. My sixth sense told me to take a trip over to her neighborhood so I could tell her how I had enjoyed the night with her. I put on a Nike sweat suit with the latest Air Jordans. Then I walked out into the neighborhood to see if I could find a crack head with a car. I noticed Fast Eddie with this white crack head man sitting in a four door Ford Explorer. They were getting high.

I walked over to the passenger side where Eddie was sitting with the glass pipe in his hand. I spoke. "I need a ride, Eddie." Eddie responded. "You got some crack. Because this cracker can't function unless he get's another hit."

"I'll give yall a gram to hit if yall take me where I need to go."

I said.

The gram was like music to their ears. Eddie had opened the door before I could finish my statement. I reached Eddie the gram to inspect it, because I knew he would be the one holding the dope. The white crackhead looked over at Eddie once Eddie got in the back seat. I got lost in my thoughts once the two crack heads started talking about how good the crack was I was selling. My mind went straight to Rhonda. It was like I had been shot in the butt with a love arrow. The little bit of time I had spent with her made me realize that I needed a Ride or Die chick.

I knew Rhonda was a Ride or Die chick but she was missing a Ride or Die dude. She really didn't talk about her past to much, but I knew about her baby daddy Dewayne and her boyfriend Jay. I knew she had to be at her mother's apartment in Westwood because she had made a statement about going to her mother's apartment to throw Jay off. When the white crack head pulled into the Westwood neighborhood, I noticed a few fiends out on the block. This wasn't my side of town, but I knew crack could get a crack head to snitch on his mother. I told my driver to pull over so I could talk to this slim, dark skinned, skinny fiend standing on Fleetwood st. "What up?" I asked.. The fiend was dressed in a one piece black disco dress that looked like she had been wearing it for the last two days. Her hair was pulled tight in a ponytail and she was wearing apple red lip stick.

"Ya'll looking for a good time?" She asked.

I spoke. "No, I'm looking for this girl named Rhonda."

"She don't work out on this block. This is my block. I do all the tricks around here." The Fiend stated.

I knew this fiend was under the influence because her speech was slurred and her breath smelled like liquor.

"The girl I'm looking for don't get high. She used to stay over here with her mother," I said.

The fiend put her hand over her mouth. She closed her eyes like she was looking for this female I was talking about. Then she pointed towards the apartment building by the semi hill up from Fleetwood St. She spoke, "You talking about Meke's sister Rhonda? They stay up on the hill with their mother Miss Pat.

"What apartment?" I asked.

"Apartment number five." The fiend responded.

I reached into my pocket and pulled out a dime rock. Then I gave it to the fiend.

"Thank you, you sure you don't want some of this best head in Da world?" The Fiend asked.

The white crackhead's eyes had gotten big when the statement had rolled off the girl's tongue. Eddie continued to pull and push at his pipe in the backseat. I answered "No. Not today."

"Well, I will hollar at yall. Don't tell Rhonda I told yall where she live," The Fiend said. Then she turned and walked in the opposite direction. The white crack head pulled the Explorer into Rhonda's mother's parking lot. I hopped out the vehicle and walked slowly to the building. The sun was shining bright making it hard for me to see the numbers on the building. I put my hand above my eyes so I could find apartment five. I looked back at Eddie and the white crack head once I found the right apartment.

Chapter 7

MARTEZ

They both were sitting in the back seat getting high. I continued on my mission towards the building after I noticed a light skin female looking out the apartment window. It was apartment five. The female looked like Rhonda but she had a lighter skin tone. I could see she was dressed in a house coat and her long hair was sticking out from under her black hair net. I walked up on the front steps. Then I knocked on the door after I recognized the doorbell was broken. This light skin female answered the door.

"Who are you looking for?" She asked.

"I'm looking for Rhonda." I responded.

I took notice of this female's beautiful eyes. They were hazel with a touch of green inside them. At first, I thought this female had on contact lenses, but when I took a closer look I could see that they were real. She said, "Rhonda is in the backroom asleep."

I almost lost focus on the real reason I was here, so I regained my composure by saying. "Can you wake her up for me?"

"Who are you?

"My name is Martez and what's your name?"

"I'm Meke. I'm Rhonda's baby sister."

Rhonda hadn't really talked about her family. I didn't know she even had a sister. To my surprise, she had an older sister too that was just as beautiful as their youngest sister. She showed up in the living room after Meke let me in. "Who are you?" Tanika asked.

"I'm Martez. I'm a friend of Rhonda's." I responded.

"Rhonda got a man." Tanika said.

Meke spoke. "Why are you all up in Rhonda's business? If you don't mind, leave Martez alone."

"Shut up Meke. You don't pay bills here. If I want to say something about who Rhonda goes with I can say it up in here because I help mama with these bills, you don't!" Tanika said.

I did not know if Rhonda's mother was here or at work. It was a weekday and it was 9:00 am according to the clock inside the two-bedroom apartment. The apartment was small with wooden floors and it had a kitchen that was the size of a closet. The living room had a couch, table, a matching chair and a small color TV that sat on an old stand. There were beer bottles all over the place. If I had to guess, it was Rhonda's mother's paraphernalia. Rhonda had told me about her mother's alcohol problem and how her mother always left bottles laying out. "Rhonda get up girl. You got this damn boy out here waiting on you." Tanika yelled.

Meke spoke. "You always got to show out. You need to find out who your baby daddy is."

"Fuck you bitch! You little whore." Tanika responded. I couldn't believe what I was hearing here. These two beautiful girls were acting out like they didn't have any respect for each other. They were acting like I wasn't even there because neither one of these girls were afraid to express themselves in front of me. They left the room. Rhonda came walking out the back room in the same Daisy duke shorts and T-shirt I had seen her in at my dope spot. She looked like she had been asleep because her hair was messed up.

Rhonda spoke, "What are you doing over here? How do you know where my mother lives?

"Well, you gave me your mother's location at the hospital and I got this fiend down the street to tell me where you mother's building was at."

"People are crazy!" Rhonda shouted.

"Why you say that?" I asked.

"He or she told you where my mother lives and they don't even know you."

"You see what crack can do?"

We sat there in silence for a moment. Then I spoke. "The reason I came is to let you know don't be leaving your earrings on my dresser." I pulled out the set of earrings I got from this crack head two days ago. Rhonda's eyes lit up when she saw the diamonds. "Those ain't my diamonds!"

"They are now. You deserve them."

"I'm no a hooker."

"I know."

I didn't know why I gave Rhonda the earrings. It was something about that moment that made me do it. My guess was it was ghetto love. "These are nice."

"I knew you would like them."

I watched as Rhonda put the ear rings on. She took her time like she was arranging herself for a special occasion. Seconds later she spoke. "Look Martez. I really don't want you to get the wrong idea about me. You know I have a relationship with Jay." I hesitated before I cut Rhonda off. "I'm not trying to take Jay's place. I just want you to know I really care."

"I think it's just my sex. I enjoy being around you and talking to you on the phone."

"I enjoy being around you too Martez, but I'm with Jay."

Rhonda turned in the opposite direction of me when she finished her sentence. I could tell she was falling for me, but her current situation with Jay was making it hard for her to really open her heart to me. I did not want to push Rhonda away so I said. "Maybe it's time I leave."

"I don't mean to rush you off, but Jay do sell drugs in the neighborhood."

"I understand Rhonda."

I kissed Rhonda on the cheek and headed for the front door. When I exited the building, I could hear Rhonda's sister cheering Rhonda on about getting the diamonds from me. I knew I made a mistake.

CHAPTER 8

RHONDA

I couldn't believe Martez had shown up at my mother's crib. It did not shock me that a crack head would give him my mother's apartment building number. I knew that crack could do things to people and get people to do things. I went back to my little bunk bed to get some sleep when I was interrupted by a knock on the front door that sounded like the Charlotte police. My sister Tanika came running in the room after Meke. Both of my sisters were out of breath. Meke spoke. "That's Jay at the front door."

"Girl, he look mad!" Tanika said.

I stepped out the small bed. Then I walked slowly to the bathroom to look at my hair and take the ear rings out my ear. By this time my sisters had let Jay inside the living room, I could hear them down the narrow hallway holding a conversation with Jay. This made me nervous because my sister Meke was always trying to play little joke on me whenever she knew she could get away with one. She was laughing from one of Jays comment when I entered the room. I had walked in slowly and said "You up early."

"I couldn't sleep knowing you was here at your mother's apartment." Jay responded.

My sisters left Jay and me alone. When I took a seat Jay joined me on the couch. He put his head on my lap. I knew instantly he could smell Martez's body scent on me. He slowly raised his head and looked me inside my eyes. Then he asked. "What have you been doing?"

"I told you I have been asleep."

"You don't smell like it. It smell like you been working out."

I knew Jay could smell the sex fluids of Martez's and my body fluids mixed. It was a loud scent because it was loud enough for him to recognize it through my shorts. I didn't know why I did not take a rag and wash between my legs while I was inside the bathroom. "I did a few jumping jacks after I took a walk to the store this morning."

"It smells like you done more than that."

Jay was right but I wasn't about to play the guilty girlfriend role. It was too early in our relationship to let Jay know I was cheating with Martez. At the moment, I had too much to lose. Jay had taken me away from all the drama in the hood and was providing for me far as my wants and my needs. I wasn't about to mess that up. I changed the subject.

"What brings you out so early?"

"I told you I couldn't sleep."

"Well, let me go freshen up a little bit."

"I like you like that. Your scent is turning me on."

I did not know if Jay was playing games or just making me sweat. The one thing I knew at the moment was I couldn't let Jay taste me with Martez's body fluids still inside me. I pushed Jay slowly off of me. He didn't protest when I reversed the role of being the investigator. "Did you sleep good last night?" I asked.

"No. Because you weren't there."

"So you were thinking about me?"

"Yea."

I was trying to keep Jay's mind off my scent. After running Jay through a ton of questions about his night without me, I said, "I'm going to take a shower and then we're going to go home."

"You can take one when we get there," he responded. I wanted to protest but I could see the seriousness in his eyes. I was a little puzzled about Jay's demanding attitude because he was always letting me get my way, but this morning he was taking charge. We rode in silence for about 15 minutes. I thought he had put the puzzle together because he had this crazy facial expression on his face. When he spoke, I listened.

"My sister likes your daughter, but she think you are a gold digger."

"Jay, she really dosen't know me. When I'm in the house with her, she dosen't even talk to me. She tries her best to avoid me when it's just me and her."

"I know. That's why I got us a crib."

"You got us a crib?"

"Yeah."

"Where at?"

"The Bahamas apartments."

I wanted to jump out my seat and hug Jay, but that would have made him think I didn't like his sister. So, I stayed nonchalant about it and continued to act like this wasn't new. "How much is the rent?" I asked.

"You don't have to worry about that. I'm going to pay all the bills. All you have to do is look pretty while I run the city."

I knew this was a new Chapter in my book of life, but I didn't know I would learn that Jay had another woman in his life. When his beeper kept going off inside the car I decided to ask Jay who was that blowing up his number. He spoke. "That just a sale."

"Damn. They want that crack that bad?"

"Yea, she do." Jay responded.

I wasn't expecting Jay to say he was selling crack to a woman.

It was ok for him to sell to a man, but a woman, I didn't trust because I knew how a woman could use her pussy to get what she wanted. I knew this because I was doing the same thing to Jay at the moment.

"Who is this woman?" I asked.

"You don't know her." He responded.

"How do you know?"

"She ain't from around here."

"Where she from?"

"You're asking a lot of questions. Why do you want to know where is she from?"

"I've got to make sure my man is telling the truth."

"Just trust me. I'm telling the truth."

I reached for the vibrating beeper after Jay laid it between the console. He beat me to the device. "Why are you so protective over that beeper?" I asked.

"It was my money machine."

"I think you are hiding something."

He spoke. "I have nothing to hide."

"Well, let me see the number?"

Jays little smile fell off his face. He thought he was being Mr. Slick. I knew Jay was cheating on me because I had found one of his condoms missing from the pack he had left inside one of his shoe boxes inside his closet. The day before I had counted the condoms after we had sex. The very next night, Jay stayed out late in which he had told me he was out selling dope in my mother's hood. The incident happened the first month I had moved in. That's why I decided to give Martez a shot of me. I went for the beeper again. Jay moved the beeper to his opposite hand while he continued to steer the rental car.

"I don't want you to get involved with my crack heads. This business is danger." He said.

"You'll let me sit at your sister's house with dope but you don't want me to know who you selling it to?"

"The less you know the better it is for me."

Jay was full of shit. He had taught me his ten rules to the crack game. Now he was trying to cover up the fact he was having a little affair on the side. The thought of the love affair didn't affect me but I was affected by Jay's untruthfulness. I watched Jay walk inside the rental office of the apartment after he got out of the car. Then I began my search. I found an open pack of condoms in the glove box. Only one was missing from the pack. I couldn't let Jay off the hook when he came out the rental office building with the key to our new apartment.

"What the fuck is these?" I asked.

"Those aren't mine. Those are my cousin Shawn's."

"I didn't know you had a cousin named Shawn."

"Yes. I had him in the car last night. He worked for me."

"You need to let me meet Shawn."

"I can arrange that." Jay said then started smiling. Jay reached me the key. Then we made our way to our new apartment.

I dropped the subject about Shawn when I walked in the two-bedroom apartment. The place was empty. But the walls were freshly painted and the kitchen had a new stove and refrigerator. The living room had a brand-new carpet that was thick with designs of different color lines with a solid black background. I fell in love with the place instantly. Jay expressed how he loved the place too. He went into details on how he wanted the living room decorated. "I'mma put a black leather living room set with glass lamps inside this room. Plus, a large screen TV."

I spoke, "I thought I was suppose to decide what I want for this apartment."

"It's up to you to pick the colors from the kitchen, bedrooms, bathroom, and the walls inside the apartment."

"I always wanted to decorate my first apartment by myself. I think you should let me."

Jay said. "You can if you let me do this." Then he reached for my button on the front of my Daisy Duke shorts. I pushed his hand away and said, "I told you I need to take a shower."

"You don't need a shower. I'll take you like that."

Jay wasn't taking no for an answer. I didn't know how I was going to get out this shit.

"I don't want you to help me get a yeast infection!"

"Girl... What are you talking about?"

"That's a lady thing! I know you know about that!"

Jay spoke, "I'm not gonna give you a disease. You know I'm clean. Shit, we been fucking without a rubber when you're not on your period."

I said, "I know but when you have sex when you not clean it's much easier to get a yeast infection."

Jay said, "I've never had a yeast infection."

"Not you dummy. I'm talking about me!" I responded.

My sister Tanika had taught me how to keep my body clean. She taught me the do's and don'ts when I first had my first period." Jay was persistent in his action to get me out my clothes at our new apartment. He came with some more punch lines that had me thinking he was not going to take no for an answer.

"This is our first apartment together. I think we should have sex right here on the carpet to welcome our new Chapter of our life." Jay was good at making things sound good when he talked and it wasn't helping that I was getting aroused from him rubbing between my legs. I spoke "Let me use the bathroom."

Jay didn't protest. He watched me as I headed up the stairs to the small bathroom. I entered the bathroom. Then I looked around for something to wash between my legs. There was a used bar of soap and a used roll of tissue. I cleaned up with these two items before I returned to Jay down stairs. He was lying on his back on the carpet with his eyes closed. I knew the routine. I positioned myself directly on his face. He stuck his tongue inside me and sucked at my clitoris like he was trying to suck the life out of me. "Ah... Ahh... Ah..." I couldn't help myself with the way Jay was eating me like he was a hungry African kid that found a whole meal in the jungle. I came on his face three times before he came up for air. Then I sucked him until he busted off in my mouth. I discovered Jay had been having sex the night before too due to the small amount of juices that came out his penis. I also discovered Jay had another girl on his team my age. I got her number out the beeper when Jay had fallen asleep.

CHAPTER 9

MARTEZ

I didn't know what had gotten into me. All my years on earth, I had never loved anyone but my grandmother. She was the only person that ever made me feel like I was important. Now, my love for Rhonda was different. You can say I was hoodwinked by Rhonda. She had literally stolen a piece of my heart with her long conversations about her childhood and what she wanted out of life. It was like I couldn't get enough of being around her. She was fun, loving, funny, trustful, and she could make love like she was doing it to make a living. It shocked me that she was so loose with the booty. When I heard she was messing around with this guy named Tank who was new in the city, I had to see why. I knew about her situation with Jay, but I wasn't going to let Tank knock me out the box. When I pulled up in North Charlotte on Belmont St. I recognized this dude named Turk who was a part of this gang called the "Charlotte Kings."

I had met Turk through his cousin Nikki whose brother was moving work for the new Blood dude who was trying to take

West Blvd from my connect Ty. It was crazy how the Kings had one side of the North Charlotte neighborhood and these Crips was moving in on the other side. I had heard through the streets Nikki was now messing with a Crip dude. My love for Nikki no longer existed and the reality of her little girl being mine was a 50-50 chance I had quit school. Nikki had quit me shortly after I had quit school. I felt like she used me for my little bit of basketball fame I had amass through playing high school sports before I quit school. I was a pee-wee when I had met Nikki Nicole Brown. She was two years older than me and had a daughter that was six months old whose name was Kenyan. At the time when I had met Nikki I was a basketball star, but basketball wasn't putting money inside my pocket. Plus, basketball wasn't stopping those white folks from the welfare office from coming to my grandmother's apartment to check up on me. So, I quit school and started selling crack cocaine for this guy named Tony Polk. Once I got into the game, Nikki moved out Dalton Village Projects and moved in with her father on 17th St. in North Charlotte. Nikki was three months pregnant when she had moved in with her father who owned a slum house in the drug infested neighborhood. It had been almost a year since I saw or heard from Nikki. I had gotten a message from her brother Scott that she had named her second little girl Keosha. I was not in a rush to be a father. Plus, I did not know how to be a father due to the fact my father didn't teach me or claim me when I was born. Nikki was past news, but the streets were talking so I decided to kill two birds with one stone. This was why I stopped Turk on Belmont St. and asked him where Nikki was at?

He said, "My cousin ain't fooling with you. You blew your chance play boy."

"What you talking about Turk?"

"Everyone knows Nikki brother Sam Brown got that work. He letting them things go for 1,000 a piece!"

I knew Turk was talking slang in codes about cocaine. This

wasn't the first time I had heard Nikki brother was the King of North Charlotte. "I don't want no dope from Nikki's brother. I need to speak to Nikki about this guy she suppose to be seeing." I said. Turk said, "My big cuz got a man. You know she go back with Willie Mcvay?"

Willie Mcvay was Nikki's first boyfriend and her first daughter's father. He was in jail doing six months for driving drunk when I became involved with Nikki. "Man, I don't care about Willie. I just need to speak to Nikki." I said.

Turk started laughing. I interrupted his little frenzy when I said. "You look broke out here. Sam must not be doing too good if you out here dressed like a bum."

Turk was dressed in an old white T shirt, dirty blue jeans and some semi new Air Jordan's. His hair was pulled back in corn rolls. He was the same complexion as Nikki. His darkish brown skin was ashy like he needed some lotion. "Look Nigga. I've been out here on the grind for the last two days. I'm making money." He said as he grabbed a pocket full of stacked up bills from his pocket.

"Turk. Turk. You out here penny pitching. I can put you down with some real work." I said.

"I'm getting mines. Trust and believe that."

"Since you don't want some un-cut cocaine, tell me where Nikki is."

"How you know my shit is cut?"

"Because I can smell the cut on the money you pulled out your pocket." I stated.

Turk looked at his stack of bills. He didn't know that the residue from the bag he held his dope in carried residue. This fool had put his money in the same plastic bag after removing the dope he had had in the bag. Dummy move. Something a rookie would do.

"Martez, you don't know what you talking about. That was just a lucky guess." Turk responded.

"You know I'm five years older than you. I stepped off the porch before you."

"Age don't mean nothing." Turk said.

"Look, I went to school with your gang leader. He used to watch me get all the girls. He looked up to me."

"You disrespecting my set?" Turk said exposing his missing teeth.

"No, I'm just trying to let you know I been in these streets."

"You lucky I like you Martez. If that lil girl by Nikki wasn't yours, I would put a cap in your ass!" Turk stated then pulled out a long Clint Eastwood chrome pistol. I gave Turk a smile. Then stepped out my rental car to shake his hand. I didn't think I was doing the wrong things since he had pulled out his gun. A pack of young gang members came running out this white house that Turk was standing in front of with their pistols out. There was five of them closing in fast. One of the guys had a A-R 15 and three of the guys had nine millimeters. The tallest one out the group had a pump shot gun.

Turk recognized what was going on and stopped the guys with a hand motion. They all returned to the house after making sure Turk was okay. Turk spoke "You see my homies got my back?"

I thanked Turk for giving information on Nikki after I had told him that the G-men started this gang stuff in Charlotte. I didn't have time to debate this issue with Turk so I gave him my beeper number and told him to call me when he wanted the uncut-raw cocaine. I pulled up at Sam Brown's little mini mart inside the hood on Pilgrim St. Sam was sitting behind the counter of the small store when I walked in. He was dressed in a purple sweat suit, Air Maxes and a Nike shirt. Standing at six-foot even with light pole looking arms and bull looking legs, Sam looked like he could be playing linebacker for the Dallas Cowboys. The store didn't have much in it. There was a section in it which there were 40's, cokes, and bottle water. The store had no fruit or vegetation. There were several other things in the store like razor blades, plastic sandwich bags, and glass pipes that had little flowers inside them to disguise the purpose of the glass pipe.

Sam spoke. "What are you doing over on this side of town?"

"Looking for your sister."

"She don't want you. You are a dead beat!"

"What are you talking about?" I asked.

I was trying to play dumb with Sam because I didn't want to fall out with him inside his store. "Nikki had a daughter a year ago. She told me you are the father."

"She has never told me this." I lied.

Nikki had called me while she was at the hospital having the baby. I had told her the baby couldn't be mines because I couldn't have any kids. She didn't get mad or debate with me about Keosha. I heard the phone go dead in my ear after I had denied the kid twice.

"Mama's Baby Daddy's Maybe."

"Dad's Maybe Mama Baby." I stated to Sam as I walked to the drink cooler.

"This isn't a game. My sister was messed up behind you." He said. Then Sam came from behind the counter with his fists balled up. Two customers entered the store with a small child in between them. This brought Sam back to reality. Plus, he had noticed the big chrome 45 pistol inside my waistline. I was dressed for action. My Air Jordan's were tied up tight and my Nike sweat suit was loosely fitted to make it easy access to my gun.

"I didn't come over here to fall out with you. I just need to see Nikki. We have some issues to clear up."

"You don't know me boy. I can have you fucked up. My money long like a porn star's dick." Sam stated.

I knew Sam wasn't going to do nothing to me in front of the two chicks inside the store. He had too much to lose and he knew I could be his niece's father. Sam grabbed his store phone after he rung up the order for the customers. Then he dialed up Nikki. He said a few words to her and called me to the phone.

"Hello." I said.

"It's been a long time Martez," Nikki said.

"I know Nikki."

"What do you want?"

"I need to see you."

"What is it?"

"I don't want to talk over the phone. I want to see you in person."

"People in hell want ice water Martez."

"I didn't find you to fight. I just want to clear things up between us."

Nikki agreed to meet me on East Way Dr. at McDonalds. I took Sam's number before I left his store. Then I placed the number in my back pocket and headed over to meet Nikki. When I arrived, I spotted Nikki sitting in a booth with both of her little girls. I still wasn't claiming the little girl by Nikki even though she was the same complexion as my mother and had a birthmark on her face like mine. Her birth mark was bigger and showed up clear on her light skinned face. She had long slim arms like mine. There was one trait that stood out the most that had me leaning towards not taking a blood test. The little girl had the same brown eyes as mines. Nikki looked like she was pregnant but she still looked the same.

I stepped over to the booth after I had ordered a number three. While we waited, I started my investigation. "I spoke to your brother."

"I know. That's how you found me."

I was trying to make conversation, but Nikki wasn't making it easy for me. "I see Keosha has gotten big."

Nikki stated "She ain't yours if that is what you want to know."

"I didn't come to fight with you," I said.

The two little girls were sipping on milkshakes. They both were well behaved at their tender ages of nine months and eighteen months. "I'm not here to play games. I really want to know if Keosha is my child?"

She asked. "Why now?"

"I need to know. You know the streets are talking."

"Willie has been helping me since Keosha was born."

"It's only right, because I helped with Kenyan while he was in jail."

"Just forget us Martez." Nikki said and grabbed Keosha and Kenyan up. She headed for the door while I watched. When she got to the door, she said. "My brother Sam is in trouble. He needs your help too." Then she put the kids in her brother's car and disappeared.

I thought Nikki and I would talk and everything would be alright between us, but the quicker she came back into my life, the quicker she had left. I didn't know her brother needed my help. It didn't seem that way to me. I was upset I didn't get the ask her about Tank since that was the real reason I had come over to the North side of the city.

My mind was still flowing with questions about this dude Tank. I wanted to find out a little information on Tank before I went at Rhonda about her little love affair with Tank. I headed back over to Nikki's brother store on Pilgrim St. It was like I was on a wild goose chase. This was the first time I had been strung out on a female like this. Sam started laughing when I re-entered the store. He spoke "the little meeting didn't turn out like it was supposed to huh?"

"No, It didn't."

The store had a little crowd inside now. Sam had some dude taking the orders while he stood next to the small back door that was in the back of the store. He opened the door. Then said. "Come back here. There is something I must tell you." I walked inside the small room. There was a wooden table, three lawn chairs, and several items of dry food stock inside the room. This room didn't look like it was used for anything but storage. But Sam showed me different. He pulled out a large package that was wrapped up in plastic with a red skull head on the front of the package. Then he tossed it on the small wooden table. Then he spoke. "I have been put on consignment."

"What are you talking about?"

"This guy came to me three months ago. He dropped like hundred kilos on me."

"That's a lot of coke."

I knew Sam was selling dope, but the amount he said was unbelievable. My connection Ty was moving bricks too, but he never told me the amounts he had going out to the public. I knew Ty had money, but he never displayed like Sam was doing. When Sam pulled a switch on the wall and the panel on the opposite side of the wall opened, I noticed a large cardboard box.

"That box have over 50 kilos in it." he said.

"I have three more months to finish them." He stated.

"What are you talking about?"

"Sit down Martez."

I sat down like Sam told me too. He put the box on the table. Then he pulled the tape loose from the top of the box.

"See look," he said.

I looked over into the box and noticed a stack of unsealed packages that were the same type of package with the red skull head that was sitting on the table next to the large box.

Sam said. "I met this dude. He's from the West Coast. I think Cali. Well anyway, I didn't ask for these kilos. He made me take the dope after he took my son from the daycare."

I responded. "Man, what are talking about?"

"This guy is a West Coast Blood. He has high rank." Sam said.

I didn't know what to say. It was like my mind went blank. All this dope had me thinking about the police. A few what ifs flashed to mind. The number one what if was. What if the FEDS run up in this store?"

"How did you get involved with this guy Sam?"

"That's a long story Martez."

"I have time. You can tell me."

I really didn't know Sam was moving work like he was SCARFACE. It surprised me that he had over 50 kilos in a box inside this store. I thought he was just like me. Selling drugs just to get by.

"This all started when I decided to go out on a job with my father for the city of Charlotte. I got the job and worked for two months before I met Roy." Sam stated.

"Who is Roy?"

"He's the high-ranking Blood gang member. I met him on Nation Ford Rd. on my lunch break. My dad was inside the store cashing a check when Roy walked up on the car and asked me for a light. He had this Cuban cigar inside his mouth and he was chewing on the end of it. I gave him a light and asked him did he know where to get some weed? He said yes."

Sam stopped mid-way through his story. Then he turned toward the door that was the entrance way to the room. He locked the door before he continued. "Roy gave me his beeper number and his hotel number then he disappeared."

"What happened next?" I asked.

"I called him about week later. I asked him if he had a pound of weed. He said he didn't sell weed. He told me cocaine was his thang."

Sam was getting emotional. I didn't know why but I was going to find out. The tears began to drop from his eyes as he continued. "I didn't want any cocaine. My whole plan was to get some weed from a different connect for a cheaper price. See, at the time, my connect was charging me nine hundred a pound. I was thinking I could get it cheaper from Roy because he was getting it from out of state. He told me he was from Texas, but I knew from his accent that he couldn't be from there."

Sam paused again. This time he pulled out a picture of his son. I knew it was Sam Jr. because when Nikki was staying with her mother in Dalton Village Projects, there were several pictures on the wall that Sam and his son had taken together. He said, "He took my son."

"Why?" I asked

"Roy, he took my son for insurance."

I played dumb like I didn't know what Sam was talking about. "Insurance for what?"

"These kilos!" Sam shouted.

I didn't understand why Roy, this gang member from the West coast would take Sam's son and make Sam sell the cocaine, then it came to me. Sam's brother Scott was like the King of North Charlotte. He was known for being a robber and a ladies' man. I knew this from running into Scott on several occasions when he came to visit his mother. Nikki was always bragging on Scott after he was released from prison. She used to tell me stories about how Scott was terrorizing the North Charlotte neighborhood. At first, I didn't believe her until I encountered an episode where Scott was standing outside the hood's club fully armed with an A-K 47, Tommy gun, and a bullet proof vest. He was looking for this guy that wasn't from the neighborhood because the guy had started trying to set up shop on Belmont St. where Scott was selling his product. I had witnessed Scott pistol whip the guy and shoot the guy in the leg for general principle. This had confirmed everything Nikki had told me about her brother, Scott. In addition, I knew Scott specialized in turning young women out. He told me out his own mouth he like them 9-99.

After I ran all these facts through my head, I spoke. "How long did he give you?"

Sam spoke "Six months"

"Or what?"

"He will kill lil' Sam!"

Sam had three more months before he had to have Roy's money. He was halfway finished but Sam didn't believe he wouldn't make the dead line without taking over the whole city. I didn't know what to say to Sam at the moment. There was nothing in the world that I wouldn't do if one of my family members were in trouble or someone I really cared for needed me to provide the money for their freedom like Sam was doing for his son. Sam was dealt a hand where he could either win both ways or lose both ways. Roy had taken Sam's son from the day care right before the drugs were delivered to Sam's girlfriend apartment in Piedmont Courts Projects. This made it hard for Sam to focus on selling the cocaine because he knew that Roy knew where all five of his remaining kids were staying at.

Roy had made it where Sam could make a little profit off the cocaine but not much since he was making Sam pay 35,000 a kilo. Sam was only making a couple hundred dollars off each kilo if he only did deals with weight. The price for an ounce of cocaine was a thousand dollars in Charlotte.

Sam had started cutting his cocaine with baking soda after he had realized he had a pure product that could hold seven grams of baking soda on every ounce of cocaine. He knew at 35,000 a kilo that it would be 3,500,000 he would have to pay Roy for the hundred kilos. At the moment, Sam had over half the money. He showed me several boxes in the room that I thought were large boxes of food but was money wrapped tight in the wraps you get from the bank. Most of the money had been exchanged into big bills in which most of the boxes were stacked with thousand stacks of hundred-dollar bills. This was the most money I had ever seen in my life. It was the same story with the dope Sam had displayed for me. I had never seen so many dead presidents in one room. My instincts kicked in. I knew that I could be kidnapped or killed inside this room for all this money. My hands and armpits began to sweat. I felt like the walls were closing in on me. At the moment, I became afraid and full of fear due to the reality that Sam was actually the black SCAR FACE at the moment. Sam spoke. "You know why I took the time to tell you what was going on in my life?"

I didn't speak. It was like Sam had read my mind for an answer.

Then he continued. "I have this cause and now you are a part of it. You know too much so I just can't let you just leave out alive."

I knew what Sam was getting at. I had saw the movie SCARFACE a million times. It was like Sam was now playing the character from the movie in real life. I was about to be a pawn in his chess game. "I need you to help me get this money. You know my cause and you know your daughter by Nikki can be a victim just like my son in this war on drugs." Sam stated.

Was I actually hearing Sam right? Was Keosha really my daughter? The two questions I had asked myself took over my brain. I didn't know if Sam was playing mind games or if I was really a father. "Mama Baby Daddy's Maybe." I said in silence, then I said "Sam, I already have a connection. I don't need your dope." I said. "Didn't ask you if you needed it. I'm telling you that you have no choice. You got to help me get my son back." He responded.

Sam was trying to do the same thing to me that Roy was doing to him.

"I got to get my blood test." I said.

"You are a fool. Why would you want a blood test and my little niece got that same birthmark like you got on the left side of her face. Her birthmark can be seen better than yours because she is lighter than you."

Sam had a major point. I had recognized this fact when I saw Keosha with Nikki at McDonalds.

"What do you want me to do?"

"Help me take over West Blvd." Sam responded.

I didn't know if this was the Bloods plan to use Sam to get me to flip on Ty, but I decided to help Sam because Keosha could be my child. Sam pulled out two kilo's and gave them to me. I took the kilos in to my hands and looked at them like they were foreign objects. I knew this was a new beginning to a new world. The more money you get the more problems, I thought. I had heard this saying before the rapper Biggie smalls made the song. After I gave Sam a number he could contact me at, I strolled out the store with the two kilos in a brown paper bag. The song from UGK echoed in my ears. "I got my first kilo from my baby mama brother."

✦ 76 ✦

CHAPTER 10

RHONDA

I met Tank at a restaurant two weeks before I had met Jay. He was dressed in a white muscle shirt, blue jeans, and Air Jordans. He had a short, faded haircut, and a stare of a tiger. His eyes were the same color of some bee honey. He introduced himself after he had offered to pay for Tori and my food. I had said. "No thank you. I don't need someone to pay for my food."

Tank looked to be in his early twenties. He was built like he had done a prison sentence. His muscles were toned and his brown skin was clear. He had this glow that would drive a woman wild. I didn't want to enter into another relationship due to the fact that DeWayne had left me before I had my daughter so I brushed Tank off by saying "I got a man."

He didn't stop with trying to get with me. He had asked Tori for my phone number after I went outside and got in the rental car.

When Tank called me two days later, I was feeding my daughter. He said. "Do you know who this is?"

"No, that's why I'm asking." I said.

"This is Tank. I met you at the soul food joint with your girl Tori." I knew instantly who this guy was, but I did not have any interest in Tank. In my eyes he wasn't my type. For one thing, he was to built up like he worked out for a living. Number two, he did not know I was only seventeen years old.

"Do you know my age?" I asked

"No. You never told me."

"I'm sweet seventeen."

Tank went silent on the phone for a moment, then he said "Tori told me you were 18 years old like her."

"I'm seventeen and a half"

"You got a body like a grown woman."

I was stacked up like some I-hop pancakes. The baby didn't do too much damage to my butt, but I still had fat on my stomach area.

"What do you see in me?" I asked

"I want to get with you girl."

"You don't even know me."

"That's why I'm trying to do. Is get to know you."

I gave Tank permission to come over to my mother's apartment. He took my offer and rode his motorcycle over and offered me a ride. I took his offer and enjoyed myself on the back of his 900 Ninja motorcycle. After riding to Freedom Park and down Betties Ford Rd. through the Sunday traffic, we ended our day at the Red Roof Hotel on Sugar Creek Rd.

I had agreed to chill out at the room since my sister Tanika agreed to baby sit my daughter. Tank had some of the best cologne I had ever smelled.

I had on one of the pair of the six pair of pants my sisters and I was sharing. My tank top was blue and it matched my blue sandals.

When Tank took off his shirt, I felt my pussy become wet. It was like the cologne and the malt liquor had changed my mind about Tank. I spoke. "Do you have a woman?"

"What kind of question is that. Do you think I would be here if I had a woman?"

I wasn't new at dealing with guys older than me. I knew how they like to play games. I played along with Tank's little game and asked "What if I gave you some pussy on the first night?"

"What did you just say?" He asked

"I don't like to repeat myself."

"You're just so blunt." Tank responded with a smirk.

"I don't like to beat around the bush. My pussy needs some work done to it, but my man is out of town." I lied.

"I thought you didn't have a man?"

"I was talking about my dead-beat baby daddy."

I was trying to keep Tank off balance. At the moment, I didn't even know where DeWayne had disappeared to and I hadn't had no sex since my six months of my pregnancy. I was now horny so I said "We can fuck." Tank went to work on my pussy like he was eating some good soul food. He was licking and sucking on my clit like he was trying to turn me out.

"That feels so good." I said as he continued to enjoy himself. I came so much in Tank's mouth that he had looked up at me with my juices on his lips. He licked his lips and went back to work. I sat there in a state of ecstasy enjoying his golden tongue. Tank really knew how to use his tongue on a woman, but when he went to my butt hole I tried to stop him.

"What are you doing nigga?" I had asked.

"Don't talk, just enjoy this."

Tank stuck his thick tongue so far up my ass that I was calling out his name. "Tank! Tank! Oh Tank! What are you doing to me?" I shouted.

He continued to serve me like a waitress serving at a restaurant. The sensation he was giving me was mind blowing. When his middle finger entered my pussy this sent me over the edge. "God help me!! God help me!! I have seen the light!!" I shouted. Tank was really doing his job with my body. He had me coming out my butt hole. This was something I had never done before.

"Please Tank. Don't you stop!" I screamed.

I had to let Tank know I was enjoying him and his tongue so I started rubbing his head with my hands. I came again out my butt hole." I'm coming. I'm coming." I had screamed again.

I had heard I could come out my ass, but when I experienced this I almost lost my mind. I wanted to feel Tank inside of me. If his tongue game was ruthless, I knew his dick game would be even more special.

"Fuck me. Fuck me." I had whispered to Tank.

He met my command. I felt his dick go inside of me after he let up on my butt hole. When I'm into my sex game, its like my emotions are caught up in the act. This was what had happened when I let Tank stick his dick inside my love tunnel. It was like we were on a roller coaster riding at full speed. "Fuck this pussy Tank. Fuck this Pussy nigga." Tank was doing me so good I almost forgot where we were. I knew the walls in the room was thin, and there were several "Do not disturb" signs on the doors of the other rooms, but I wanted to come all over Tank large pole, and I did. He came next! He let his man juices spill inside of me on purpose because I told him I was on the pill. He went limp after several more rounds of my good love tunnel. I had to suck on the head of his penis just to get him back in the mood. We 69'd for about a half an hour before he re-entered his huge cock back inside of me. He was going so fast that I thought I busted off twice before he did once. After he slipped out of my love tunnel that was filled with my hot juices, he slipped his penis in my butt hole, again! "Ah! Ah! Ah!" I had shouted every time he drove his huge cock in my butt hole. It was like he was stretching me to the outer limits. He had some good dick. His dick had tasted like my love juices after I had hopped off of it. I super sucked his dick till it turned purple from my lips and throat. This episode had ended when Tank came down my throat. I had drained his balls as I sucked the juices out of him. He had curled up in the bed like an infant after we finished and this negro was sucking his thumb like a baby. Like I said. I had met Tank two weeks before Jay. The one night stand I had had with Tank left him craving for me. The only reason I didn't crave for him was I asked him about being a gang member and he had said. "No, I'm not a Crip." I never asked him if he was a Crip. He gave me this information without me doing some real investigation. He had told on himself from the very start. The information I had gotten from Tori only confirmed my assumption I had about him. He had lied so I never gave him a chance. Tanks motorcycle was blue and the bandannas he had tied to his handle bars represented his flags. I didn't know much about being in a gang, but I knew Tank was in the Crips due to the knowledge I had gotten from Snoop Dog. I called Tori after having my flash back of the one night stand with Tank. She stated. "Tank has been asking about you girl. That fine mother fucker was at the club doing wheelies on that motorcycle of his. When you gonna let me take Tank for a spin?"

"You know that golden rule. We don't fuck behind each other." I stated.

"Girl, I was just kidding." Tori said. Then she started laughing that stupid laugh of hers. She was always getting under my skin with that crazy sound she made with her voice when she make when she thought something was funny.

"You know you sound like a damn rooster." I said.

"Forget you Rhonda. I hope you didn't call to talk shit."

Tori and I had been friends since we were kids. She was a year and a half older than me, but it didn't make a difference. We had met when she came to West Wood with her brother when crack first hit. Instantly, we became friends because our parents were all addicts in some form or fashion. We had attended the same middle school, Carmel Junior high. Tori had quit South Mecklenburg High after she found out I was pregnant. Her reason for quitting was unknown to me until I caught her selling her body for money to pay her mother's bills. Tori and I became grown over night. She had her own apartment in which she was letting her big brother stay there because he didn't have anywhere to go when their mother moved back to New York. Tori was 19 and I turned 17 after moving in with Jay and his sister. It was like we were made to be best friends. We had so much in common. Like for instance, I loved me some good sex, money, guys and family. She did too. We both loved men in general. We were in between when it came to color. I could deal with a boy if he had money, but Tori could get on their white's level even if money wasn't involved. She knew how to talk their language.

"No, I didn't call to talk shit. I just wanted to remind you to shave your hair off the top of your lip." I said. I knew this would get on Tori's nerves.

"Forget you hooker!." she shouted.

"It takes one to know one."

"I know two."

"You and Meke."

"I'm not a hooker!"

A few seconds went by before Tori asked, "What do you want Rhonda?"

"I need Tank's number." I said.

"I thought you was off that one-night stand."

"I want to ride his motorcycle again." I stated.

"You so nasty. I thought you only let him eat the poo na na?"

"I did. Plus some other things." I said

"Like I said, he's been looking for you. He said your body is calling his name."

"R. Kelly right?"

"Yes, the album, bitch".

"Well get his number." I said. "I got it its 375-9418."

I took down the number and put the paper in my dresser drawer where my panties were at. I did this because Jay never went inside this drawer. Then I told Tori to lose Tanks number.

She said "Imma keep it. Just in case things don't work out with you two." I hung up. Then I dialed up the number I had taken from Jay's beeper earlier. A female answered. "Hello?"

"Who is this" I asked.

"You called me!"

"Is Jay there" I asked.

Jay got on the phone. "You busted nigga!"

Jay didn't deny the fact he had another young woman when he got home. He tried to brainwash me by telling me it was all for his drug business. But in my opinion, Kendra had Jay too. He spoke. "Rhonda, I don't care about that girl. I just sell dope out her apartment."

CHAPTER 11

RHONDA

Who is this girl Jay?" I asked.

"She ain't nobody special. I had met her when I went to North Charlotte to get my money from my cousin Shawn." Jay stated.

Shawn was Jay's cousin on Jay's mother's side.

"So, Shawn introduced yall?" I asked.

"Some thing like that. It wasn't for sex."

"So you fucking this bitch?" I asked.

I was curious about Kendra because she was trying to move in on my turf.

"No, not really." Jay answered.

"What do you mean, not really?"

"The plan was for me to get in where I fit in. Then set up shop," Jay paused.

"But what Jay?" I asked.

"The girl started liking me. Plus, her baby daddy got two years in prison."

"So, you gonna play baby daddy to her child like you do mines?" I asked.

"It ain't like our relationship. I told you, I'm selling cocaine out of her apartment."

I wanted to slap Jay right in his face, but I kept calm and let him run his little bullshit ass game on me. "So, what am I suppose to do if I see ya'll together?" I asked Jay. Jay started laughing like something was funny. I didn't think what I said was funny because I really wanted to know.

"She knows about you. I told her everything." Jay stated.

"What the fuck are you doing sitting around talking to this bitch about me for?"

"I don't want any conflict. That's why I explained to her about her position."

"Who the fuck do you think you are?" I responded in my ghetto voice.

"Like I told you. I have a team. You are one of the stars on it. You have an important role. Please Rhonda play your position and don't asked too many questions. "So, I suppose to sit around here and let you cheat on me?" I asked.

Jay didn't answer right away. It was like Jay was letting me know he wanted his cake and his ice cream too.

"It ain't cheating. I'm just doing what I have to do to hustle out of her apartment." Jay responded.

"You can find another apartment for that. There are lots of crack heads running around in North Charlotte."

I poked my lips out and folded my arms across my chest. Jay took my gestures like he always did. He knew I was mad.

"Once I get in good, I will look for a better apartment in the hood."

"What are you saying Jay?" I asked.

"Imma sell there until something come open."

"Or until you find some more pussy around the hood you can stick your little as dick in." I said.

"Don't start with me Rhonda." Jay shouted.

"You know your dick is small." I stated in a ghetto fashion. I knew Jay had a complex about his dick.

"You're the only one that say that." Jay said.

"Well, you must be messing around with some kids if they say your dick big." I stated.

Jay looked like he was getting mad. He balled up his fist like he was getting ready to fight. I said. "You gonna hit me because your dick is little?" Jay didn't respond.

"Little dick. You mad at me?" I asked.

Still Jay didn't respond.

"Don't get mad because God didn't bless you with enough to please a woman." I said.

As my last word came off my tongue, Jay grabbed me by the throat.

"Why you always teasing me about the size of my dick?" He asked.

I couldn't breathe. It was like time was at a standstill. My feet were dangling in the air. I was seeing stars.

"You can't talk now?" Jay asked.

I couldn't talk because this fool had his hands wrapped around my neck. He was cutting off my wind.

"You don't appreciate shit. You're always complaining about something."

I had been nagging Jay lately. In other words, I had been getting on Jays nerves. He loosened his grip a little bit. Then he let go. Jay continued "Out of all things, you want to complain about my dick size? You could have continued to pretend like my dick was big enough for you." I spoke. "I'm not good with acting Jay. See, acting is for people on TV"

Jay said. "It's always a smart comment with you. Why can't you just play your position and shut up?"

"You want me to continue to act like you don't be hurting my feelings?" I asked.

Jay didn't respond. He turned his attention to bagging up his dope. I walked over in front of him and asked. "That's what you want Jay?"

Jay continued to put the small rocks in the plastic vials. He repositioned himself on the bed.

"Now you're giving me the silent treatment?"

Jay didn't say anything.

"Sometimes I feel like you ain't man enough for me Jay. You act like a little boy." I said.

Jay said. "Didn't I take you out the ghetto.?"

"This place ain't too much better."

Jay said. "It's a step up from where you were."

"You act like you got me living in a castle. You ain't no king."

"You sure ain't no Queen."

Jay hadn't never been disrespectful like he was at the moment. This was all new to me. I had caught him at the girl's apartment but I never caught him talking on the phone to any kind of female in my presence.

"I give you the crown for little dick king." I said.

"There you go again. Making jokes about my dick."

"It's not a joke. It's the truth."

"Then why are you still here?" He asked.

I hesitated, then spoke. "I ask myself that same question every day. It's like I can't come up with a good answer."

Jay said. "I can answer it for you. It's because you mother is an alcoholic and your daddy is a crack head."

I said. "What my parents got to do with this?"

Jay didn't respond. He just continued to stare me down.

"Answer me Jay!"

Jay turned in the opposite direction and went back to putting the rocks inside the vials.

"That's what I'm talking about. You can't be man enough to finish what you start." I said. Then I turned to walk away. Jay grabbed my arm and pulled me towards him. I struggled to get out of his grip.

"I don't want to fight Rhonda," he said.

I could feel his penis getting hard up against my leg. He looked me directly in the eyes and said, "I love you, girl." I didn't know what to say. It was like I was lost for words. My tongue was stuck and my heart wasn't in to this little moment Jay was giving me.

"Do you love me Rhonda.?" Jay asked.

Like I said, I wasn't in love with Jay bit I did have love for him because he was taking care of me and my daughter.

"I don't know Jay." I answered.

"You don't know?"

Jay didn't take this answer very well. I could see in his face he was disappointed from my answer.

"I love you Rhonda. You got me going all soft up in here"

I really didn't want to fuss and fight with Jay. The only thing I wanted to know was where we now stood.

"I got love for you Jay." I responded.

I knew it was up to me to play my position or me and my daughter would be back in Westwood fighting for a bunk bed and a piece of the welfare check my mother was receiving on my daughter's behalf. I didn't want this because I had become used to sleeping in a nice warm bed with a man to lay up with. There was other stuff I would miss if I had to return to my mother's apartment, like the money Jay was giving me to go shopping with. Plus having my own space. I wasn't about to give all this up or let another young tender take my spot. It was time for me to put in work and reclaim my position. Since Jay's sister had taken my daughter with her to the beach, I knew I didn't have to worry about any interruptions. When I sprang into action, I knew this would surprise Jay since I was on my monthly cycle. He knew I didn't like to have sex while I was bleeding, but my position was in jeopardy so I had to do what was essential to gain ground on this trick that was trying to move in on my turf. I put my tongue down Jay's throat to start off the fore-play. He kissed me back.

We floated into a wave of passion until Jay broke off the kiss and asked "Aint it that time of the month?"

I engulfed with Jay again. He broke off the kiss again.

"You know Imma want some pussy. So why are you doing this to me?" He asked.

"Imma give you some." I said with a wicked grin.

"But you on your period."

"This will be new to the both of us." I stated.

Jays' eyes lit up. I knew Jay was a freak. He was always trying to slip his dick up my butthole during sex. I had always protested because, after that one-night stand with Tank, my asshole was sore for weeks. I could take Jay up my ass, because he was only a mere six and a half inches. I knew this because I had taken a 12-inch ruler and measured it. It hadn't taken me long to finish the task of measuring Jay's dick after that night of hard fucking. I hadn't gotten the full effect because Jay was small like a baby and quick like a bunny rabbit. That was why I had measured him while he was asleep. I pulled the top off a bottle of lotion. Jay looked up as I poured some on my fingers. Then I dropped the Daisy Duke shorts I was wearing. My asshole was in view of Jay's vision now. I passed him the lotion after he slipped out of his shirt and shoes. Then I positioned myself over him with my crack to his face. It looked like I was about to ride a horse backwards. In Jay's case, a small pony. Jay used his fingers to rub the lotion over my tender ass hole. Then he dipped his middle finger inside my ass after I did the same. Jay was breathing heavily as he swirled the lotion onto his dick and lotioned up his mere six-inch dick. Then he got on his knees behind me. He licked my ass before he positioned himself back on the bed on his back. I straddled him backwards slow rocking down on his cock. "Holy shit," I groaned. Letting my upper body collapse onto my crossed arms on the bed. When Jay was all the way in me, I felt the head of his cock actually twitching deep inside my guts. Then Jay started pounding me, sliding his slippery cock in and out my incredibly tight ass hole. It felt like he was touching my tampon. The two of us were groaning and grunting like a pair of jungle animals in heat. I was expecting to feel the same feelings I felt with Tank, but to my surprise Jays dick was perfect for my asshole. It was completely different feeling from when Tank fucked me. Even if the mechanics were basically the same, the size changed the whole nature of the sex. I was totally focused on feeling Jay inside of me. Every thought and emotion was on pleasing Jay. I could feel his dick spurting so I clamped down so hard on Jay's dick I came with him. His come was hot and juicy thick. It seemed like he had shot sparks all through my body.

"Girl, you always bringing something new to the table every time I think you have done it all." Jay said.

Then he gave me a kiss in the mouth after he slid out of me. The room smelled like pure sex, but I didn't care. I had done what my duty had called for. I made my man bust the most powerful nut he had ever busted. It was like he lost all his super powers when he had gotten up because I had him eating out my hands after our anal incident.

CHAPTER 12

MARTEZ

It had been shocking to me that Nikki's daughter looked like me. This shocking truth changed my mind about finding out about this guy who Rhonda was having sex with. I was now a father of a beautiful brown skin little girl who really didn't know I was her biological father. The truth of the situation was, I really didn't know for sure but I my whole mind set had changed after my conversation with Nikki's brother Sam. I knew Sam needed my help to get lil Sam back because I knew these Blood Gang members were serious. They had already proven that when they took half of West Blvd. There had been several people killed because of these Blood Gang members. The Bloods had taken over several crack heads' apartments in several neighborhoods on other sides of the city. These Blood Gang members were changing the city right before my eyes. It was like I could see clearly now, because of the wars that were going on in the streets. I had taken the dope Sam gave me back to my dope spot and put the product on the market. The fiends liked this product better than Ty's product because it was purer.

The fiends ran for a week straight. In other words, they wouldn't stop beating the door down until the last rock was gone. The whole time I was selling Sam's product, Ty constantly kept trying to get in touch with me. He had sent people to my dope spot, but I never answered the door because I knew Ty had sent these people. I wasn't hiding from Ty; I was just trying to help out Nikki's brother because I felt like my daughter by Nikki could have been in lil Sam's position, too. I decided to give Rhonda a break too. It had been a week since I had talked with Rhonda, or enjoyed some of her freaky sex. I decided to call her after I gave Sam his $72,000.00. I had to call Tori to get in contact with Rhonda because Rhonda and Jay were staying together off Freedom Dr in an apartment. Tori called Rhonda on three-way after I stated my business. Rhonda answered on the third ring. "Hello."

"Rhonda girl you won't believe who I got on the phone." Tori said. I could hear the surprise in Rhonda's voice when she said "Who Tori?"

"Martez" Tori responded.

"So he's on the line?"

"Yes, I am." I responded.

"Is it ok for you to talk?" Tori asked.

"Yes. Jay is in the shower." Rhonda said.

I didn't like this creeping around stuff, but this was the only way to talk to Rhonda until she could find a way to let Jay down without breaking his heart. I knew the whole story about how he had gotten shot while they were walking to the store and I knew Rhonda felt like it was her fault he was semi-blind in one eye. That's why I had agreed to wait on her.

"When can I see you?" I asked.

"You the one that been dodging me." She said.

"I had some stuff I had to take care of."

"More important than me?" She asked.

I could hear Tori on the phone while Rhonda and I held a conversation and this made me feel like I was a kid.

"You know, you are the apple of my eye." I stated.

"Keep that game Martez. Use that on a bitch that dosen't know any better." Rhonda said.

"I don't have a bitch," I stated.

She said, "I know you don't have one bitch, you got bitches."

"I told you I've been busy. I had stuff to do." I still could hear Tori in the background laughing under her breath.

"Listen Martez, I ain't slow to the game. I know when a nigga is cheating on me." Rhonda stated.

I was a sucker for love. Was I really in love? Was it just lust? These two questions had popped to my mind while Rhonda went on and on about me cheating on her. Here she was staying with Jay and having sex with him whenever he asked, but was making me feel bad about cheating on her.

She was the real cheater. I didn't feel like I was cheating on her because I was on a date with the streets. The streets were more than sex. There was money to be made other than sticking my dick in a woman. I had girls that gave me the eye and there were also crackhead hoes that enjoyed sucking on me for rocks in my neck of the woods, but I didn't like that. I had fallen for Rhonda. It was something about this girl that had grabbed my attention. I wanted to make her my wife and get the house on the hill with the kids and the dog. After Rhonda's little speech, I spoke. "When can we meet. I need to feel you girl."

"You're still thinking with your dick Martez. You're not thinking about my feelings." She said.

"It has only been a week, Rhonda."

"I know but I was worried about you. I thought something happened to you. You know what I've been through with Jay." She said. Rhonda was always using her and Jay's situation to make me feel bad about not answering her calls. It always worked too.

"Look, I'm not Jay. I want you to stop thinking bad stuff

when you can't get in contact with me." I said.

"I can't help it Martez. I love you." she said.

I could still hear Tori breathing on the line. It was like she was enjoying the conversation that Rhonda and I were having. She was making gestures and that told me that she was liking what she was hearing.

"You know how I feel Rhonda." I said.

"You can't say it." She said

"Girl, you know my heart." I shouted.

"Well, say the three little words."

I didn't like to show affection to anyone while people were around. "I'll say when I see you tonight." I responded.

"I ain't coming if you don't say it." Rhonda said with her ghetto attitude.

I really didn't want to show Rhonda affection with Tori on the line, but I was weak to the V-shape. "I love you." I said.

Tori busted out laughing. This made me mad because I knew Rhonda was only doing this to impress Tori.

"I might come over tonight." she said.

"Girl, you better bring your butt over here." I said.

"I'm still mad at you. You know you were wrong for not checking in." She said.

"We're not married Rhonda."

"You're still my man." She said.

"Just say homie lover friend." I retorted.

I could tell something was wrong when I called Rhonda's name after she didn't come back with a witty comment. When Tori spoke, that explained it all. She said, "Jay must have come in the room."

"I can't keep playing these games." I said.

Tori said, "You are the butt naked man!"

"What is the butt naked man?" I asked.

"All women have one of these. You just happen to be Rhonda's Butt Naked Man. Plus, you already said you love her. That was so cute!" Tori said. I knew Tori was trying to get under my skin. It was just in her blood to get on my nerves. The first time I had met her, we were on the phone and she had something smart to say. It was like she was laughing at me for being a sucker for love. "Well, tell Rhonda to call me when Jay goes to sleep." I said.

Tori broke out laughing again. I know she was laughing at me not with me. In her book, I was a sucker because I was getting Jay's leftovers. When Rhonda arrived at my dope spot, I was putting up another two kilos that I had collected form Sam on co-signment. I wasn't going to let this sex break get in the way of helping Nikki's brother. I opened the door and rushed out and paid the cab. Rhonda was dressed in a pair of Daisy Duke shorts, T-shirt, and bed room shoes. Her hair was wrapped in a black scarf. I wasn't into kissing, so I moved my head when Rhonda tried to kiss me on the lips when I stepped through the door. I spoke. "Don't do that. I know you had your lips on that nigga's dick before you got over here."

"No, I didn't. I didn't even have to fuck him tonight. He just fell asleep."

"A lie dosen't care who tells it."

"I didn't come over her here to play games Martez. I came over here so you can fuck me."

"Maybe I don't want any right now. I'm tired of being your butt naked man."

Rhonda busted out laughing.

"What's so funny?"

"Tori said that to you?" She asked.

I turned in the opposite direction and grabbed a box of blunts I had purchased from the store earlier. Then, I busted a blunt while Rhonda continued to laugh at my comment.

I said. "I don't see anything funny."

"You need to stop feeding into what Tori says."

"I feel like a sucker." I said.

"Martez. You're no sucker." Rhonda stated and then started

laughing again.

"It's time you make a choice."

"What are you saying?" she asked.

"Either me or Jay?"

I pulled the bag of weed out my pocket and then I emptied the sack into the blunt. I knew Rhonda didn't like the smell of weed. She was always complaining about Jay smoking weed in their apartment. "What are you doing?" She asked.

"Imma bout to get high as hell." I said.

"You know I don't like weed."

"Well, you going to have to put up with it tonight." I said.

I continued my quest to finish rolling the blunt. Rhonda pushed my hand causing the weed to fall out the blunt onto the floor. "Girl, what's wrong with you?" I asked.

Before I could get the weed from the floor, Rhonda was stomping on the weed. In her emotional state, she started crying. I could see the tears falling from her eyes. "What's wrong?" I asked her in a sterner voice.

"The smell reminds me of when my mother's boyfriend used to molest me." she shouted.

This was shocking news to me. Rhonda had told me she was molested, but I didn't know the smoke of weed could trigger off a reminder of her episodes. I didn't even get to add the light to the blunt before she went into her frenzy. This was all new to me. Seeing Rhonda having this panic attack made me realize how drugs had a cause and effect on people. I embraced Rhonda to calm her down from her attack. She fell in to my arms sobbing like a child in its mothers' arms. I kissed her face and said. "Everything is alright."

After I got Rhonda back to her normal state, I called Tori and told her about the incident with the weed. Tori told me to put Rhonda in a cab before the sun came up. I did what Tori said. Before the cab arrived, I tried to get Rhonda to talk. She only answered to yes and no questions. After she answered several questions, I helped her into one of my jackets and told the cabbie where to drop her off. "Camp Green St." I said. I watched as the cab pulled away from Farmer St. In my mind I knew I was dealing with a young woman that had been mentally damaged. I didn't know at this point what our relationship would end up being but the incident with Rhonda had shown me how drugs affect people on all different levels.

CHAPTER 13

MARTEZ

The little episode with Rhonda made me realize that drugs affect people mentally and physically. After Rhonda got back to her apartment, she called me. I didn't know if I should have answered the call because she hadn't never called me from that number before. I answered. "Who's this?"

"This is Rhonda."

"Are you alright?"

Rhonda hesitated. Then she spoke. "I have been wanting to tell you the whole story about when I was molested by my mother's boyfriend."

I didn't say anything. I just listened.

"I was nine years old when I started getting my monthly cycle. At the time my mother had been a alcoholic for about two years. My daddy had already left her and my sisters. Times were hard. So my mother let Willie move in. He was from the hood. He drove a cab. At first he was nice to me and my sisters. Then one day he just flipped."

I continued to listen without making any comments while Rhonda went into deeper details about her childhood.

"Willie came home after driving all night. My mother had gotten a part time job cleaning at this school. My sisters were at school, but I missed the bus because I had woken up late. That day, I was at home by myself lying in my bed when Willie came into my room. At first, I thought he was just checking to see if anyone was in the apartment, but he walked back out the room and came back in naked."

I could hear Rhonda voice starting to tear up.

She continued. "He stood over me at first with his dick in his hand. I laid there like I was asleep. He jacked and squeezed at his dick while he looked over in between my legs. At the time I was on my period, and I had never had a dick inside of me or knew anything about sex."

The tears were falling now. I could hear the fluid from her eyes hitting the phone. She continued. "I thought it was strange that Willie was jacking his dick in my presence because I had heard him and my mother having sex on several occasions. I never actually saw them in action but I knew how sex sounded." A crack head knocked on the door interrupting Rhonda and my phone conversation. "Hold on a minute Rhonda." I said. I put the phone down. Then I looked out the top window in my play sister's apartment. I could see Fast Eddie standing on the door step with a guy dressed in a black hoodie, black jeans and black shoes with a gun to Eddies back. I didn't say a word. It took me a few seconds to get Rhonda off the phone before I headed down stairs with my gun in hand. I opened the front door. Then I exited the apartment. Eddie was still knocking on the back door when I cut the corner. The guy didn't see me coming. I let off one shot. I could see the flames from the gun as it had exploded. Then I watched as the guy hit the ground. "Ohh shit!" The guy in all black said. Eddie took off running, and I was left there with a guy bleeding at the back door step of my dope spot. The guy had dropped his gun when I had shot him in the back. The gun was lying on the ground about three feet away from him. He was in pain, and blood was everywhere. "Who sent you?" I asked.

The guy was lying on his stomach with his arms and legs spread out like he was being arrested by the police.

"Please don't kill me." He begged.

"Who sent you nigga?" I asked.

I was dressed in my army fatigue pants and shirt. I had a pair of black Air Force Ones on. Plus, I had a black bandanna wrapped around my mouth with an all-black white sox hat on.

"Nobody sent me," He said. My rage came to a boil.

"So, I can kill you and nobody will know?" I asked.

"Please man." the guy begged.

I reached down and grabbed the gun. Then I walked over to the guy and kicked him in the face numerous of times. Then I stomped his hands, legs, feet, and his face. The guy passed out. I thought he was dead. My rage subsided. Then I remembered Eddie had ran off.

It was now five am in the morning and I was out looking for Fast Eddie just in case I had to take his life. I knew if the police put pressure on him he would snitch me out. I ran through the projects like I was hunting for animals in the jungle. I had both guns out and ready to shoot. In the distance I could hear a fire truck and an ambulance. My search for Eddie didn't last long. I decided to hop in my rental and leave the hood. It took me 20 minutes to get to Freedom Dr. where Rhonda said she would meet me at an all-night gas station. Rhonda came walking up Freedom Dr. with her arms across her chest. She was dressed in bigger shorts, a t shirt, and some bedroom shoes now. Her hair was now pulled back into a ponytail. She quickly entered the car, and I didn't say a word until I hit Billy Graham parkway. I pulled into the Red Roof Inn. Then I said, "I hope you're not gonna get into any trouble on my behalf."

Rhonda smiled. I thought it was best not to tell Rhonda about the shooting incident at my dope spot. I paid for a room for two nights. Then I gave Rhonda the key. She took the key and went up to the room. The sun was rising as I pulled out the parking lot to enter the store parking lot across the street. I entered the store and purchased a package of rubbers, soda, two breakfast sandwiches, and a pack of cigarettes. I didn't even smoke cigarettes. I purchased them because I knew I could not smoke weed in front of Rhonda. When I entered the room, Rhonda was laying back on the bed watching the news. I put my items on the nightstand and offered her a sandwich and she spoke. "No thank you." I fired up a cigarette. Then I asked. "You ain't hungry?"

"No, maybe later." She responded.

"So, you gonna stay a while?" I asked.

"Jay will be up around 12 noon."

"You put him out like that?" I asked.

"Don't start Martez." She said.

Rhonda cracked a smile. I knew she was still having sex with Jay. It was best I played along like I didn't know. That way, I could continue to get the pussy anytime I wanted it. I could see Rhonda still had something on her mind. She could tell I had something on mine too. "Are you alright Martez?" She asked.

"Yes, why do you ask?"

"Because when you called me back after I told you don't call that number again you sounded like you were in trouble." This girl was already learning how to read me.

"I just wanted to make sure you were alright. The weed incident had me thinking." I said.

"I tried to finish the story, but I was interrupted by your little dope fiend." she said.

"You know that is how I take care of myself."

"I understand Martez." she said.

A news flash caught my attention. I noticed my dope spot on TV, and I quickly turned off the TV and lit up another cigarette. I blew the smoke out my mouth after I had pulled the cigarette to ease my nerves. "Why did you turn off the TV?" Rhonda asked.

"I don't like the news. They get everything wrong."

"Damn, you smoke?" Rhonda asked.

"This ain't gonna make you get all insane like you did earlier at my dope spot?"

"Cigarettes don't cause my panic attacks. Just weed."

I knew I touched a nerve when I brought back up the subject of her panic attacks because Rhonda made a crazy face expression.

"So, I'm safe?"

"It ain't funny." Rhonda said. Then threw a pillow at me.

"I'm sorry. I really do want to know why weed do you like that."

"If you want to, I can finish telling you right now."

Rhonda took a deep breath and went back into her story. She started where she left off about Willie, her mother's boyfriend standing over her with his dick out. "He masturbated on my leg. His juice from his dick was thick and warm. I just laid there pretending to be asleep. After Willie took a rag and washed off his manhood juices off of me, he rolled up a joint and took a few pulls off of the joint. I knew what weed was because I had seen him and my mother smoking weed before. I took a few pulls after Willie threatened to tell my mother that I had stayed home from school. He knew this would get me to do anything because he knew how much I feared my mother. The weed took a while before the full effect hit me. But when it did, I was so high I didn't know if I was coming or going. I believe Willie put something other than weed in the joint because I seen how weed made people hungry or made them laugh a lot. It didn't do me like that."

I said. "What happened then?"

Rhonda hesitated then said. "He taught me how to suck his dick. He liked it fast and sometimes slow. Then he fucked me while I was on my period. I was only nine years old. Willie knew his dick was too big for me."

Rhonda busted into tears. I knew I had reopened a wound that she was trying to let heal.

"It's over Rhonda." I said as I crawled up in the bed and hugged up with her.

"He put something in that weed." She shouted.

Rhonda rested her face in my shirt and I could hear the hurt in her voice. I had problems of my own at the moment. It was crazy how I was able to listen to Rhonda's story but I couldn't build up the courage to tell her what was going on in my life. I wanted to tell her about Nikki and Keosha, and also about the two kilos I had helped Sam get rid of and the 2 kilos I had gotten from Sam after I had moved the first 2 kilos.

I wanted to tell Rhonda I owed Sam $72,000 at the moment and I had just shot a dude in the back lot of my dope spot. I also wanted to tell Rhonda about how Ty was looking for me and how I started a war between Ty and the Blood gang members. I was carrying around so much stress that I knew if I didn't release it, I would blow a gasket. It didn't take me long to get Rhonda out of her clothes. I was in her like a thief in the night. This was something we both needed.

"OOOHHH" She moaned as I entered her pussy. Pleasure rippled through my body as I slowly rammed my love muscle into her love tunnel. I could tell from her moans and gasps that Rhonda was enjoying it too. "Is it good Martez?" She asked.

"You know its good baby." I responded.

I pushed my dick up inside her until I could feel the bottom of her ocean. It felt like I had a million soft hands massaging my dick. My orgasm took about two minutes to boil before I exploded inside of her.

"Damn... Damn..." I said as I busted off. I wasn't finished yet. Rhonda wasn't either. She sucked on my dick savagely and left it hard and wet before she got on all fours on the bed. I watched as she glided my dick in her pink asshole. "Oh my God." She screamed out in pleasure. I watched as my dick disappeared into her asshole. It was tight around my whole dick. Once she got the whole dick in her she threw herself back at me as I pumped inside of her. "Yes! Yes!" She whispered into the air. She was making love faces that were turning me on. She flashed this wicked smile that told me she was enjoying herself. Her contractions wracked against my dick and became stronger and stronger the faster I went. I knew she was on the edge of busting a nut. Then it happened. I felt Rhonda's juices engulfing my dick. It was wet and sticky warm. The whole bed was wet from our sweat and love juices. I enjoyed myself but my problems hadn't gone anywhere.

CHAPTER 14

RHONDA

November 1997

This was my 18th birthday. I want this to be one of the best days of my life because I now had money to spend. My past two birthdays were spent with Tori and my sister Meke drinking 40's on the front steps of my mother's apartment building. Jay decided to let me spend some time with my girls because he had me stuck up in our new apartment for weeks. It was like he had me on house arrest and he was my house arrest officer. Tori and Meke told me to meet them on Woodlawn Rd. at this gas station so we could hook-up. They had a big surprise for me but they did not want Jay to see it. Jay dropped me off at the gas station where Meke and Tori were waiting inside Tori's boyfriend's Mustang. Jay made a few mean mug faces at both my sister and Tori then he took off in the opposite direction we came in.

I was so excited about seeing my surprise that my sister and Tori had for me that I had forgotten to wear my underwear.

When they stepped out the car to give me my birthday hugs, I asked, "Where is my damn surprise?"

Meke responded, "You have to wait until we got to the hotel room and where are your underwear?"

"I left them and what hotel?"

"The one Tori and me went half on so we could show you a good time." My sister responded.

It did not take us long to get to this hotel room in which there was loud music coming from the room when we had arrived.

"Who is in that room?" I asked

"A couple of thugs from the West coast." Tori replied.

"So, you went out and got some thugs for me?" I said as I point to myself.

"Yes. We want you to have a night to remember." My sister said.

"They're going to love that dress." Tori stated.

I had purchased myself a black and gold dress that was hugging my body like a cup holder holding a cup. My matching shoes were Gucci with straps that wrapped around my calves. I had my hair done by my cousin Tanya five hours before I met up with Tori and Meke. My manicure and pedicure were two days old but fresh. In my eyes, I looked like a million bucks and felt like it too. Tori was dressed in a black dress in which its exposed all her corners and curves. She had on a pair of heels and her hair was pulled back in a ponytail that reached to her upper back. Tonight, Meke was trying to be the decent one out the group. She was hiding her body under her outfit because she didn't have butt. She was dressed in white slacks and white blouse with black low cut heels. Her hair was in a long ponytail with a black ribbon tied around it. My sister Meka was beautiful to me and I was jealous of her light skin in a good way. When these thugs opened the door to the room I instantly smelled smoke. I could see there was a room filled with guys around my age dressed in Red T-shirts, blue jeans, and red shoes. All five of these guys had on red hats that had a big letter B on the front of them.

"Welcome to your party." This cute brown skinned guy said as we entered.

My panic attack no longer existed. After discussing my problems with Martez about why I was having attacks, it was like the conversation we had had helped cure me. I said "This is nice. I can't believe y'all thought of me. I don't deserve this."

The room was dressed with balloons, signs of "Happy Birthday" were all around the suite. There was a small bar with beer, liquor, and sodas by the huge bathroom.

Meke said "You deserve everything here. It's your Birthday." My sister was right in a sense. It had been a long time since I had someone throw me a party. The last person that threw me a party was my mother and she was drunk. My sister Tanika had helped pay for that party after she had received some wreck money after her school bus was in an accident. That was when I was 10 years old. My sister Tanika didn't like to party with us. She was more of a home body person. A good time for her was sitting on the front steps at my mother's apartment building drinking a 40 ounce of beer and playing a game of spades.

It didn't surprise me that Tanika wasn't with Tori and Meke when they had picked me up. I still decided to ask my sister Meke were Tanika was at. She said "She's at home. You know she has Earl over there. Mama is out of town with her new boyfriend." I knew my sister was at home getting her brains fucked out of her head. She had a huge appetite for sex like our mother. My guess we all got this trait from our mother and she had gotten it from her mama. I began to mingle with the group of guys, and it did not take me long to learn their nicknames. There was "Cheese man, Big baby, Cool-C, Yellow boy, and Dawg. Cheeseman was the shot caller of the group. Every time he snapped his fingers, the guys met his every request. He was three-hundred-pound, light brown skinned, with a bald head like the greatest basketball player to ever play the game. All the guys call him their OG but

I didn't know what OG really stood for until Meke pulled me to the corner of the room and told me that he was the leader of their gang. Meke said "Look Rhonda, this guy Cheese man is their big homie." I interrupted her. "Look lil sis, I don't care what he is. I just want to have fun and get back home safe."

"Stop worrying about Jay. He dosen't know where we are at."

"I'm not worrying about Jay. As a matter of fact, I have someone else on my mind." I said then gave Meke my sneaky smirk.

Tori cut in the conversation "Look you two. These dudes got a little bit of money. They trying to spend. What yall gonna do?"

"I ain't gonna do nothing. I told yall I ain't fucking unless its Jay."

"You know I'm all about my paper. I like nice things too Rhonda." Meke stated. I knew my sister Meke was coming into her own, but I did not want to be a part of her fake sex operation. I also knew her and Tori were out tricking dudes for money and I knew sometimes they were put in situations where they had to run off or call the police on the dudes they had stolen money from. It was wrong what they were doing but I knew they were not going to stop until someone got hurt or killed. It was just in both of their nature to get money. After I held conversations with all five guys, I decided to pair up with Yellow boy. He was 6 foot even with a physique that looked like he did some years in prison. His skin was light almost like he was a white boy and he had this wavy hair that was cut short. We were partners for most of the night. He couldn't keep his hand to himself after he had recognized that I was semi-intoxicated. "Girl, I want you." Yellow boy whispered in my ear. I flirted around with him while the other guys watched. I grabbed on his penis and kissed it through his pants. The guys went wild. It was funny how time had passed when you were having fun. After several games of spades and a game called "Shot for shots," I was incomprehensive. My sister and Tori didn't know that these guys had planned to get us drunk and have their way with us. I didn't know either until I felt one of these guys eating out my pussy like he was at an all you can eat spot. My guess he was paying me back from the little display I put on earlier with Yellow boy. I didn't know I had passed out. When I opened my eyes, I tried my best to regain my composure but I was too far gone. At the moment I felt dumb, deaf, and blind. The reason I was feeling these emotions was because I was tied up by my arms and legs to the king size bed inside the suite. Plus, my eyes were covered and my mouth was gagged. The music inside the suite was still loud and the words to the song was hard to understand because of my mind state. I tried to tune the music out to see if I could recognize the voices inside the room, but I was too intoxicated. My eyes were covered with a large white towel which made it difficult to see anyone. I started praying and asking God for help. I prayed the same prayer I use to pray when my mother's boyfriend used to come inside my room and rape me. "Please God take away this pain." At the very moment I felt helpless, and I didn't like the feeling of the unknown. Especially when I didn't give the guy my permission to touch me. I could hear two people fussing over who was next with me. Then I heard a semi fight. Then I felt this huge body on top of me forcing his dick inside of me. I was already wet from one of the dude's mouth earlier. So, it slipped right in. I could feel the dude enjoying my insides, and he was touching every wall with his large penis. It was like he was poking around for a hidden treasure. Finally, he was through with me. Then came another. He was like a jack rabbit. It took him three minutes flat before he explored inside of me. I counted every second just to try to think about something besides what was happening.

After the third dude finished, I was sure I was going to die. I had seen most of their faces and Meke and Tori did too. I didn't know if they were dead or tied up like me. The last dude took his time with me, and I could tell it was Yellow boy because he wasn't forcing himself inside of me. It was like he was doing it to please his gang members. He whispered in my ear. "I don't want to do this." I laid there and listened to Yellow boy's heavy breathing as he pounded away at my pussy. I could also hear the guys cheering him on after he had finished and stood up and walked away. At the moment I was wishing they would just take my life. I had been violated in a way I wouldn't wish on anyone. Having five guys run the train on me wasn't fun. Especially when you don't know even know them. When I was finally untied, I was shocked it was a maid in the room. My instincts told me to call the police, but I called Tori's apartment. She answered the phone on the third ring. "Hello" She answered.

"What happened to yall last night!" I shouted.

"What's wrong Rhonda?" Tori asked.

"Those guys raped me!"

"What are you talking about?"

"They raped me Tori!" I shouted again.

"Calm down Rhonda. Meke and I are on our way." Tori stated.

Tori and Meke arrived an hour later. They were dressed in their same outfits, but now had scarfs on their heads. "Rhonda, last night was your choice. You told Meke and I that you wanted two guys at one time," Tori said.

"Y'all know I was drunk. Plus, I think those guys put something in my drink!" I shouted. My sister and Tori looked at each other like I said something wrong.

"Rhonda, you drank five beers and you took about ten shots of gin. You told Meke and me you wanted to be with Cheeseman and Yellow boy. We left you with them." Tori said.

"I don't remember, but what I do remember is I was tied up and raped." Rhonda shouted.

"So, you saying those other guys came back?" My sister asked.

I shouted "They all raped me. They took turns fucking me with no protection."

My sister embraced me as I began to cry. Tori joined the embrace. I didn't know if I should call the police because I had been drinking out of control. Instead, I called Tank after I took a shower. He told me he would pick me up. My sister and Tori told me they would try to get those gang members real names so I could take out charges. I decided it was best to leave that issue alone since I had agreed to stay behind with Yellow boy and Cheeseman. Plus, I felt the same way when my mother's boyfriend molested me, which I felt like it was my fault, too.

CHAPTER 15

MARTEZ

I listened to the voicemail Rhonda had left me on my pager. There was a sense of agitation in her voice. This disturbed me. The reason was because I had missed her call. I could not distinguish what type of fear Rhonda was under due to the fact she was talking in a whisper and she was crying. I called the hotel's number back in which the front desk clerk told me that the customer had checked out at 12 noon. I looked at my watch. It was 1:00pm. I knew it would be hard to contact Rhonda at this time because she was usually with Jay during the afternoon hours.

I put on a sweat suit and a pair of Jordan's. Then I headed out in search of a new spot. It didn't take me long before I ran across a deal on Ross Ave. It was two blocks from the projects I was selling my dope in. I had found a two-bathroom house that was on the market for rent. This house was a block away from Val's old house. It didn't make a difference that the house was close to Val's old house because I was only renting the house so I could sleep in it. I had Val's boyfriend put the house in his name because he knew the rentman. It didn't take me long to get the house furnished and set up the way I wanted it. The same day I was moving my clothes in the house, I noticed this guy I looked up to. His name was Jimmy aka Creep. He was at the hood store with his brother Buff. I admired Creep because he had been a stone-cold junkie and now he had access to some weight. His name was heavy on the Blvd. Now his brother Buff was a different story. He used to be the man before he was in a high-speed chase with the police in which he suffered a head injury when he wrecked his Benz on the South Carolina and North Carolina state line. Buff was now semi-retarded from the wreck and he was hooked on crack cocaine. Him and his brother had reversed their roles. Their story gave me motivation to never try cocaine. When Creep stopped me at the store, I was on my way to purchase some sandwich bags and razors so I could bag up the rest of the dope I had gotten from Sam.

He spoke. "What's up Martez?"

I said "Nothing much Creep."

Creep was skinny like a tooth pick, and his skin was sand brown and he had these big eyes like he could look through your soul. He was 6'2" about a hundred and sixty pounds. His hair was cut short in which he always kept his New York Yankees hat on his head because the Yanks were his favorite team. Buff on the other hand was fat, and he had gained the weight after his injury. Creep still treated him like he still had a stable mind. Creep often let Buff ride with him on dope runs. Creep told me this usually kept the police from having any suspicion that he had dope in the vehicle and most of the time he had the dope inside a book bag on his retarded brother in the vehicle.

Creep spoke. "There is this young lil tender in the store. She is pretty but she is a baby."

I asked. "What are you talking about Creep?"

The female came walking out the store with a bag in her hand as I walked up on Creep and his brother sitting in their rental car.

Creep said "That's her." This female was bow legged, 5'3" pecan tan, big butt, hazel brown eyes, long hair and sassy at the mouth. I had come in contact with her before at the basketball court in Dalton Village Projects when she first moved in with her aunt. That day, I was shooting basketball and this little girl that looked like a mirror image of the pecan tan female was standing on the side line. In fact, this was the pecan tan female's sister.

I spoke. "I know her."

Creep said. "You don't know that fine ass girl."

Then he smiled. I could see Creep had added another gold crown to his mouth giving him two on his front teeth.

"That's my young tender." I said.

Creep said "Stop lying nigga."

I had to let Creep know I was a player. In the hood, where we're from you had to be a player or you was considered a square. I put my mack game down and found out Andrell was a virgin. That day at the basketball court she gave me her phone number and a month later I busted her cherry. I spoke. "I'm the first to ever hit that."

"I know you're lying. You know you haven't been in between them juicy legs." Creep said.

"Watch this."

Andrell's eyes looked like they were about to pop out of the sockets when I called her name. She turned in my direction.

"Come here." I said.

She smiled and then she walked over slowly like she was shocked that I was talking to her out in public. She asked "What do you want Martez?"

"I just wanted to see how you were doing?"

"I'm doing fine."

I had paid Andrell a visit two nights before this encounter. We had had sex in her room while her Aunt Peggy was at work. I asked, "You still my girl?"

"Yes."

Then she broke into smile exposing her braces. This was Andrell's only flaw. I dismissed Andrell, and then I said, "You see? I told you. That's mine."

Creep said. "You are a lucky son of a bitch."

"Go head on with that shit. That's my wife."

Creep spoke "Boy, I wish I was young again."

I asked Creep for his number after he told me how lucky I was to have a pretty young lady like Andrell. Then I took care my business inside the store. I returned to my new house to be met by my grandmothers boyfriend and Nikki. Nikki was dressed in the latest fashion from GAP. Her hair was done in Sprits with a little bit of red dye. She stepped out the rental and said. "I have something to tell you."

"What is it?" I asked.

She started crying. Then she said, "They indicted my brothers."

RHONDA

Two hours earlier…

I was upset that Martez didn't return my call. I had left several messages on his voice mail. After leaving him the messages, I had called Tank. When Tank arrived at the suite, Meke and Tori was sitting in the common area. I walked out the restroom and took a seat beside Meke who was sitting on the love seat inside the room. Then I spoke. "I need yall to leave."

Meke and Tori knew I was talking to them. They grabbed their pocketbooks and headed out the door. Once Tank and I were alone, I spoke. "I didn't know who to call. That's why I called you."

I broke out in tears. Tank knew something was wrong because I went silent when he asked. "What's wrong?"

I didn't know how to tell him about the incident that happened the night before. The five guys had violated me and I was suffering mentally and physically. At the moment, I wanted revenge on these guys but I didn't want them to go to prison. I wanted them dead. I knew Tank could help me with this situation. He was in the Crips and he had rank inside his set. I knew with his rank that he could rally his troops to go on a mission. The mission would be to take revenge for the pain I had suffered at the hands of the Bloods. I knew it would be essential to plant a seed inside Tank's head so I could get him to do my dirty work.

I spoke. "Something happened last night."

"What happened?" Tank asked.

Meke and Tori had already cleaned up the room. The evidence of a party was nowhere in sight.

"I was raped." I said.

"By who?" Tank asked.

"By five Blood members."

"How you know they were Blood members?"

"They all had on red."

Tank asked. "Do you know their names?"

I hesitated then spoke. "Yellow boy and Cheeseman."

"Are those the only two you know?"

"Yes," I answered.

Tank embraced me like I was his girlfriend. Then he let me know that he would handle the situation. I didn't know how I would repay him if he killed the Bloods. At the moment I was perplexed about what had happened to me and I felt like their deeds would go unpunished. All five of the Blood members had violated me in a way I had never thought I would be violated. I was under the influence of alcohol and I think the Blood members put a date rape drug in my drink. "Can you drop me off at Tori's apartment?" I asked.

"Sure." Tank said.

I knew Jay was going to be mad at me, but I called him anyway when Tank dropped me off at Tori's apartment. He answered our apartment phone on the first ring. He asked. "Why you didn't come home last night?"

"I spent the night at Tori's crib" I responded. Tori, Meke, and I had already created a story while I had waited on Tank to come to the suite. I knew Jay was going to come with some mess about he came to Tori's apartment in the late hours of the night and we weren't there. Jay said "I came to Tori's apartment. No one answered the door." I didn't want to say the wrong things so I let Jay go on in his rage so I could find out how much he knew about my night out. He continued. "I came over Tori's apartment twice. The first time I came her brother answered the door. He told me y'all had not been there. That was around 2:00a.m. Then I returned at 6:00a.m. He didn't answer the door that time."

Jay had me in a corner. I wanted to come out and tell him the truth and tell him about the crime that had taken place against me. But something inside me told me I would lose Jay if he knew the truth. I spoke. "Jay, Tori's brother lied to you. I was lying in Tori's bed around 2am."

"You're lying Rhonda. I can hear it in your voice." Jay said.

I continued to protest my case "I'm not lying Jay. I was here. You're probably are the one that's lying. You probably was out with that girl again."

Jay shouted "Cut it out. Don't try to reverse game. I know you wasn't there. Tori's brother let me inside Tori's apartment to use the restroom and I glanced in both rooms on my way to the restroom. I did not see a sign that you had been there or was there." Jay was starting to put fear in me, because I did not know he was a semi-stalker. He had always taken a sniff at my underwear when I returned from a trip over to my mother's apartment, but he did this in a playful manner. I knew he cared for me and my daughter but I never thought to the extreme of coming out in the late night to see if I was where I told him I would be. This gave me the impression that he didn't trust me so I used this to turn the attention off my unfaithfulness.

I asked "So you don't trust me Jay?"

"It ain't that I don't trust you. It's the people you were with I don't trust." He said.

I knew Jay knew how my sister and Tori operated. He knew

they were selling their bodies for money. I had told him this fact one night when we were pillow talking. "You're talking about Meke and Tori." I responded.

Jay slammed the phone down in my ear. I knew he was upset with me. I had lied and I had cheated on him by letting myself get to drunk to fight off the Bloods.

CHAPTER 16

RHONDA

Two weeks later

I thought Jay was going to be mad when I returned from my little trip from the store. He was washing the rental car out front, when I stepped out of the Nation Cab. He gave me a smile. I spoke. "You gonna take this bag."

Jay grabbed the bag without questioning me. This confused me because he was always up in my business. There were a couple neighbors outside sitting on their porches and washing their cars too.

I made my way to the apartment to be met by my sister Meke. She was standing in the kitchen in some tight shorts, a t-shirt, Air Max Nikes, and she was cooking breakfast. I did a double take to make sure what I was seeing was real. Then I said, "What the hell are you doing over here?"

"I caught a cab. I thought we could go to the mall child." Meke responded. Then gave me a smile.

"Didn't I tell you don't come around Jay with that tight stuff on." I said.

My sister continued on acting like she was really into cooking the eggs she had in the pan on the stove. I asked. "You can't hear?"

Meke spoke. "Quit tripping Rhonda. You know I don't want your man."

"You don't know if he dosen't want you."

Jay smiled and disappeared back outside. This notion gave me the impression that something might have taken place while I was gone.

"Meke. I know you didn't fuck Jay?" I asked.

Meke hesitated "No Rhonda!"

Then she gave me that weird smirk like she does when she does something she dosen't have any business doing. Before she could get another word out her mouth, I was on her like white on rice. I punched her in her light skinned face and she screamed out in pain. "What did I do!?" Then she grabbed her face, and I grabbed my sister's long hair and pulled it like I was trying to pull her brains out. She grabbed my hair, but I managed to bite her hand. She released my hair, and then she reached for my face. She managed to scratch my face and hit me in the mouth before I grabbed her finger and bit it. I tried my best to bite it off. Meke screamed. "Jay! Jay!" This little bitch was screaming Jay's name like he was her man. I continued to put a whipping on her, and I beat her for the old and the new. Jay came running inside the apartment out of breath. I could see a crowd was forming around the front of the building after Jay had grabbed hold to me. "Stop, Rhonda." Jay shouted.

I was still pounding and scratching at my sisters pretty little face when he had entered the room.

"This is a nasty bitch." I shouted.

I knew how Meke operated. She was my sister. If money was involved, she was down for whatever.

"I didn't do anything Rhonda." Meke shouted.

Jay was in between us now, but we still had each other by the hair.

"Let her go Rhonda" Jay yelled.

I could tell he was getting mad.

"Tell this nasty bitch to let me go." I said.

I was really in the wrong because I was insecure about my relationship with Jay. I was now showing my ass because I had caught my sister inside my apartment in sexy tight clothes, and cooking my man breakfast at that.

"Rhonda, I told Meke to come over here. She called around 11:00am and I answered the phone. I told her it was okay to come over." Jay said.

I could see the crowd out front of the apartment building. It was like a mountain hill of ants standing together. I spoke. "She knows I told her to never come over here unless I'm here."

"I don't want Jay!" Meke shouted.

It was crazy how I was acting over Jay. At the moment, the money was good and the sex was okay. I didn't want my sister to come in between that. She had her motives with most men she came in contact with. Especially if they weren't married. Meke spoke. "Rhonda, I would never do you like that."

I had seen Meke and Tori switch up with guys. They were young when they did it, but that memory always stuck with me. It was hard for me to share Jay. This nigga was doing everything for me.

"Get the hell out Meke." I shouted as I let go of her hair. Meke was in tears when she walked out the door. I shouted "Don't come back, you nasty bitch!."

In my heart, I felt like Meke had fucked Jay. I didn't have any proof at the moment but I knew how my sister operated. Jay closed the door and left me in the apartment alone. I couldn't believe he ran out the door after Meke. I felt like my world was falling apart, and it was like I was trapped in the closet with my emotions. When Jay returned from taking Meke home, I was standing in the kitchen cleaning up the mess Meke and I had made during our fight. Jay didn't speak. He gave me the silent treatment for about a hour. Then he spoke. "Rhonda, I know you think I had sex with your sister, but I want you to know I would never do that." I didn't say a word. At the moment I was playing back the moment of Meke cooking my man breakfast in her tight outfit. Jay continued "I'm not like you Rhonda."

"What do you mean?" I asked.

Jay said. "I know about the dude you been creeping off with."

"What are you talking about?'

Jay said. "Don't play dumb with me."

"Jay, I'm serious. I don't know what you are talking about."

Jay turned his head in the opposite direction and pulled out an old pregnancy test I had used after I came home from being with Martez.

"What is this?" He asked.

"I don't know." I said.

"I'm not a woman. I can't use this." Jay said.

I knew I was busted. It was like all of my lies and manipulation were coming to the light.

"Jay. I really don't know who's that is." I lied.

Jay placed the pencil like device on the table in a napkin. Then he took a seat and smiled. I could see every white tooth in Jay's mouth. It was like he was mocking me with his facial expression because he knew I was lying.

Jay spoke "You know you the only female that been staying here."

I nodded in agreement.

Jay continued. "I haven't had no one over here."

I hesitated then said. "Maybe Vanessa left that over here when she picked up my daughter."

Jay shouted "Bullshit! You know this is your test!"

Jay had put some fear in me when he had shouted. It was like he knew I was lying. Jay spoke "Well someone is pregnant."

I didn't say a word. I looked at the positive sign on the test before I placed it back down. Jay spoke again "Is it you, Rhonda?

I responded quickly "No Jay. I'm not pregnant."

Jay grabbed the test and walked over to the garbage can and tossed the test inside the can. Then he made this face like he was trying to get under my skin. I asked "What's with the face?"

Jay said. "I'm happy you ain't having a baby."

This statement shocked me. Jay had never told me he didn't want any kids.

I said "So you're happy?"

Jay responded "Happier than a faggot with a bus load of dicks."

Jay was always trying to be humorous.

"So do you believe me?" I asked

I knew I had asked the wrong thing before the question had left my mouth. Jay responded "I want you to know I'm leaving you Rhonda." I was confused by Jay's statement. I had asked him if he believed me about not being pregnant. It was like he had already made the choice of leaving me before he finally said "And yes I think you're pregnant."

I was in fact three months pregnant, and my stomach was starting to show. "Jay, you can't leave me." I said.

"I know I can't leave you. That's why you have to leave my apartment." He said.

I knew the pregnancy test was evidence against me in Jay's case, but I was still confused that he would have any doubts about the baby in my stomach. Then, I thought about the time he had spent with my sister Meke.

"What did Meke tell you? I asked.

Jay put his face in between his hands. He looked like he was saying a prayer.

"So, you got your information on me? Where did you get it?"

Jay looked up and said "Meke told me everything."

"What do you mean she told you everything?"

Jay hesitated then spoke. "She told me how you have been seeing that dude Martez and the guy Tank. Plus, about the five guys that raped you."

I couldn't believe my ears. My sister had violated the Girl Code. We had agreed that we would never tell one another's business to a boyfriend. I spoke. "I don't believe Meke told you Jay. I believe you read my diary."

My diary had been missing for the last week, and I didn't know if I misplaced it or left it in a cab on my way to visit Martez. Jay said. "Rhonda, I know everything. Every little detail. Every little sex episode you had with Martez and Tank."

I said. "Why, did you steal my diary?" Jay cracked a smile exposing his white teeth again. Then he spoke. "You can't keep anything from me. You know I made you. Without me you would be nothing."

I wanted to slap Jay for his comment but instead I said. "You didn't make me Jay. My mother and father did. You just took me out of the ghetto."

Jay said. "But I didn't take the ghetto out of you. You ain't shit Rhonda." Jay paused then continued. "In my book you're nothing but a whore and always going to be a whore."

Before Jay could get the whole word "Whore" out of his mouth again, I slapped him in his mouth. He responded by punching me back in my mouth. Then we tussled and fought inside the kitchen before we were finally interrupted by the police.

I had two black eyes and a busted lip. Jay had a few bite marks and a handful of scratches where I had grabbed his face with my nails. A white officer with a bald head took Jay out the door in handcuffs before I had noticed Det. Bailey standing in the common area of the apartment. He was dressed in cotton white shirt, Black slacks, and loafers. He asked. "Why are you and Jay fighting?" I wanted to disclose all the information on why Jay and I were at war, but I decided to see what Det. Bailey had on his agenda. I asked. "Why are you here?" Det. Bailey pulled out a photo line up out his briefcase. Then he placed the document in my face. Instantly, I noticed Cheeseman and Yellow boy. Then I noticed Martez was in the lineup. Det. Bailey spoke "Do you know any of these people?" I shook my head no. Det. Bailey then asked. "Are you sure? Because I think the guys that shot Jay are in the photos. "I wanted to tell Det. Bailey that I recognized Yellow Boy and Cheese man but I couldn't bring myself to do it. I was afraid they would send someone to kill me if I snitched on them for raping me.

The rent lady walked inside the apartment. Miss Webster interrupted us and said "You broke the rules, Rhonda. You and Jay have to go." I didn't want to hear this at a time like this. I had just been caught by Jay and I had just recognized the guys that shot Jay and raped me. Now I was on the verge of being back at square one. I watched as Miss Webster who was dressed in a pants suit outfit, dress shirt and heels walk out the apartment. Then I watched Det Bailey say a few words to the police who was planning to charge Jay before they all left the scene.

CHAPTER 17

MARTEZ

I knew I had to relocate after Nikki informed me that her brothers and eighty other people from the North Charlotte neighborhood had been picked up in a round up by the FEDS. I knew it was best to move out of the city since the FEDS would be looking for all the people that were getting cocaine from Sam. They had labeled Sam as a kingpin and they hit him with the Rico Act for his part in the drug conspiracy. I called my cousin who had moved to Pageland, South Carolina and informed him that I would be coming down to cool out. He knew the Street code in which I had already gone over with him before I gave him the money to rent a house in the small town of Pageland. It was like he owed me a favor for the good deed I had done by giving him the money to start his life over. When Nikki and I reached my cousin's house he was standing in the front yard cutting wood. My cousin James had the house hooked up with new furniture and the yard looked like he had just finished cutting and trimming the trees. I spoke to James and walked inside the two-bedroom house. Nikki was right on my heels as I explored the kitchen and the bathroom. After my tour, I removed several stacks of clothes out the trunk of my car, then I checked my cell phone. Rhonda had left over twenty messages on my phone. Nikki didn't say a word about me checking my messages until she heard one of my workers talking about her brothers.

Nikki interrupted. "Who the fuck is on that phone?"

"Chill Nikki. Ain't nobody talking about your brothers."

Big Boo had seen Sam in handcuffs on the 6:00pm news. Big Boo had been at my dope spot on several occasions when Sam had dropped by to check on me. Then there were times when Big Boo had helped me count out the money I had to pay Sam. I ended my phone conversation with Big Boo after he told me that Scott in which this was Nikki youngest brother was snitching. When I turned around after I ended my call with Big Boo, I noticed Nikki was holding her hands over her eyes. She was crying and mumbling something under her breath. I couldn't understand what Nikki was saying until she had removed her hands from her mouth.

I asked. "What's wrong with you?"

"You don't understand." Nikki said. I pushed on to get some answers out of Nikki. I said "What's really wrong?"

Nikki continued to cry and fumble around with her hands. It was like she knew her brothers weren't going to get out of the drug charges unless they became federal informants. Nikki and I had witnessed people in the past that were big drug dealers that had gotten in trouble with the FEDS and later became federal informants. I didn't know what to say to Nikki to get her to talk to me. It took over a hour before she opened up to me.

Nikki spoke. "Scott is going to snitch. He just got out from doing seven years at a state prison in Raleigh, North Carolina."

I didn't know what to make of Nikki words. In my book I knew I hadn't done any deals with her brother Scott, so I wasn't worried about him saying anything about me to the FEDS, but on the other hand I knew Sam could get me some foot ball numbers if he provided information about me to the FEDS. At the moment, I was so afraid what Sam would say that my nerves were a wreck. My hands were sweating and my stomach felt like I had so much gas inside of it that I couldn't stop farting. I didn't know how much Nikki knew about Sam's operation, but I had to reveal what I knew so I could get what I was looking for.

"Nikki, your brother Sam was in some serious shit. Sam was getting cocaine from the West Coast and this Blood took Sam Jr. from your brother and made your brother sell the dope for him. He threatened to kill Sam Jr. if Sam didn't go along with his plan." I said. Nikki looked at me like she was perplexed. Then she said. "That's why my brother Sam told me to get in contact with you. I have a key to his stash house in which the Blood Roy gave my brother the house."

Nikki pulled out a door key in which there were two other small keys on the key ring. She pushed the keys in my right palm before she said. "Sam said everything at the house is yours, but he wants you to take care of his wife and I."

I didn't know if Nikki was telling the truth, but I knew there had to be more than one motive behind her giving me some keys to a house where her brother was stashing his product. The first thought popped to mind was a set up. I knew how the FEDS worked. Looking back on all guys that had gotten picked up in my hood on federal charges back in "91" in which most of them that were charged in the Fed operation that was labeled: The Flood Organization back in '91' and started snitching on each other. The only real nigga out the bunch was my friend Carlos, who went to trial and received seven sentences of life after his so-called friends hit the stand on him. I put the keys in my pocket. Then I looked into Nikki's eyes. She stared back at me in which this set off a spark between us. It had been almost two years since I had been involved with Nikki. I didn't know what I was getting myself into but my Uncle Lonnie who was serving two years in

State prison for selling drugs had schooled me about women. I replayed his five rules in my head. Rule number one: Never tell a woman you love her unless you really love her. Number two: Never fall in love with a whore. Number three: Never be a fool for a woman. When I got to number three, I realized that Nikki wanted me to be her fool. It was the same approach Ty was taking in which he wanted me to sell his dope on consignment and take all the chances in the heart of the streets while he sat back and collected the money. After Nikki gave me the keys, I wanted to throw the keys back in her face, but me being who I was in which I was curious about what Sam left at the house, I didn't.

I made sweet love to Nikki without a rubber and I even broke several of the rules my uncle taught me about women. I broke the rule of telling Nikki I loved her in which I did not love her. After our night of love making, the next day we headed back to Charlotte in search of Sam's stash house. When I reached the Plaza Extension Rd. I made a turn in front of Grainger High School. Then I took the small piece of paper Nikki had in her hand that had the address to the stash house on it. I pulled up right in front of a house that looked like someone had set a blaze to it. There were items like couches, chairs, lamps, beds and TVS lying out in front of the house. Everything looked like it had been cooked on a grill, and there was a Cadillac and a small sports car that also suffered because of the blaze to the house. I looked at Nikki and then I said "Someone beat us here." Nikki began to cry again. I had pulled away from the crime scene with the intentions of finding out what happened. I knew the streets would be talking. Especially if someone had done this on purpose. I could tell Nikki was upset by her body language. She had her legs pulled up to her chest and her arms were wrapped around her legs. I watched as she rocked back and forth in the passenger seat of my car. I could tell she knew she would be moving back to the Projects, because there was no money for her to continue to live in the apartment Sam had put her in. I stopped by Soul Stack, a black restaurant on Tuck Rd. and grabbed Nikki and myself a soul food meal. She nabbed at her food a while before she finally closed the box. Then she said. "Martez, do you really love me?"

I didn't want make matters worse by saying the wrong thing to Nikki so I lied again. "You know I love you."

"Well, why you call me Andrell while you was fucking me then?"

I didn't know I had said Andrell's name while Nikki and I was having sex. This was new to me. "What are you talking about?" I asked.

"You know damn well what I'm talking about. You said that little bitch name while you was slapping my ass."

I couldn't remember exactly every little detail about the night before, but I knew one thing. Nikki was still a drama queen. I tried my best to brush Nikki off by telling her she was tripping, but that only added fuel to the flame. She said. "You love that young bitch. She must got some good pussy huh?"

"Why are you worried about her pussy?"

"I knew you were lying to me when you said you were in love with me. You think your ass got all the sense, but I knew you was planning to play me out the dope my brother had at the stash house."

Nikki was right. I was planning on getting the dope from her and then let her down easy, but plans don't always go accordingly so I had to change up my plan. When I found out I would not be receiving any dope or money, it helped me out of my commitment to her. This had given me a reason to drop her off and keep it moving, but I knew I would have to deal with her because my daughter, Keosha. I had given Nikki my promise of taking care of her and Keosha before she even stepped out of my car on Belmont Ave. She smiled and slammed my passenger door, and it was like she respected the game I tried to run. I knew she was in love with that guy Willie. In fact, she had told people that we both knew from the hood that she was in love with Willie, that and having my daughter Keosha was a mistake. Nikki was good at teaching me lessons because she was everything, I didn't want my wife to be. Rhonda on the other hand was different too, but I knew she was evolving into the same type of money hungry bitch like Nikki. Now Andrell was a different story. She was dumb by street life standards, but she was a good young woman that could be taught and molded into the woman I needed by my side.

After analyzing my situation with these three women, I decided I would stick with Andrell and play on the side with Rhonda. On the other hand, Nikki would only be entitled to money if Keosha needed anything and this agreement we had decided on had a flip side to it in which we would let Willie think Keosha was his daughter due to my lifestyle.

CHAPTER 18

RHONDA

I knew why Jay had left me. He had found my little book that I wrote down all my life secrets in. At first, I was convinced that my sister Meke had told him about all my episodes with Martez and Tank. It was funny how I had to go to my sister and ask her for her forgiveness because she did not snitch on me. Jay had lied on Meke because he was mad about the fact I had been raped and did not tell him, and the fact I was pregnant. After I moved back in with my two sisters and my mother, I put in for a section eight housing unit. I was approved three months later. It did not take long before Jay and I were back into a relationship again. We were still fighting and cheating on each other. Then a light came on in my head. I had had enough. I was at a crossroad. My in-house money man did not respect me anymore and I was six months pregnant now and did not know who my baby daddy was. So, I put Jay out. Martez did not want anything to do with Tank, but we were still friends. He had caught Tank and I leaving a hotel on Nation Ford Rd. He had this chick named Nikki that

Tank knew form North Charlotte with him that day. I found out that Nikki was in fact Martez's baby mama. Tank gave me this information after I gave him some super head. I called Martez after I had finished up with Tank. He answered my call at his dope spot on the third ring. "Who's this?" He asked.

I knew Martez's voice.

"This is Rhonda."

Martez hesitated before he responded. "What do you want player?"

"I didn't call to fuss and fight with you Martez."

"What the fuck you want?" He asked with an attitude.

I hesitated and then said. "I want you. I miss you."

"Rhonda. You know you tripping."

I knew my emotions were like a roller coaster at the moment. I had gone through a whole season of crying and laughing over stuff that I should not have had to go through. It was like my hormones were going crazy. I spoke. "I'm thinking about leaving Jay for good."

"I don't believe you." He said.

I couldn't help myself from seizing the moment. I had to make Martez feel sorry for me.

"Jay, beat me up again."

"Why you keep going through that stuff with him? Why you keep letting him put his hands on you?" he asked.

I knew I still had a place in Martez's heart.

"I don't know what to do. That's why I called you." I said.

I knew how smart Martez was when it came to separating his personal problems from someone else's. He was tender at heart but far from a push over. It was like he could sense when I was lying or faking a story.

"Rhonda, you know Jay and you will be back together tomorrow." He said.

Martez was right. My heart was tender for Jay because he could provide money for me. I spoke "I felt a little jealous when

I saw you with Nikki. You baby mama.”

I knew I had caught Martez off guard with my statement. “What the fuck are you talking about.”

“Y’all were at the room playing house. Don’t forget I saw her get in your car before you rolled up your windows.”

Martez didn’t deny the fact that someone had been in the front seat of his red Acura Legend coupe.

Martez said “Girl, that was my cousin.”

I said “You don’t have to lie Martez. We don’t go together.”

Martez was making major money now. Word on the streets was he was moving two kilos a week now. Plus, he had two apartments and two baby mamas, but he was still lying to me about these facts. Martez retorted. “I’m glad we aren’t a couple. I would have been put you in the ground, Rhonda.”

“You got jokes.” Martez let off a laugh. I knew Martez was trying to change the subject so I got right back to the matter at hand.

“Nikki must have some good pussy because she got to be seen with you during the day.”

Martez responded “Why are you asking about Nikki’s pussy? That’s her business.”

“I thought that was your sister in the car. I knew you was lying. You don’t have to lie to me.”

Martez hesitated then said. “Why the fuck you calling me asking me about other women? Do I call you and ask about who you fucking?”

I couldn’t do nothing but laugh at Martez’s comment. He was right. I was violating the player code. “You right, I shouldn’t be worried about who you sticking your dick into.”

Martez spoke. “I think its best we be friends because I don’t need any drama in my life. It’s like every time you call, it’s drama.”

“That is the way you think of me, Martez?”

“Yes, you know how to get under my skin.”

“You know this baby got me going crazy. I can’t do what I

want."

Martez said. "That should be a sign."

I knew exactly what Martez was saying. At the moment I want to hear it out his mouth. "You having that baby?" Martez asked.

"What the fuck do a baby have to do with a sign?"

Martez had cut in. "You need to slow your ass down. That's what the baby got to do with a sign."

Martez made sense. The baby could have been a sign from God.

"I got to take care of me. Ain't nobody going to take care of me like I do." I said.

I didn't want to fuss and fight anymore with Martez so I changed the subject.

"Can you come get me Martez?"

"For what?"

"I just need to see you."

I knew sex was always on the agenda for Martez. He didn't care if the time was daylight or dark. Most of the times with me were after dark. That made me come to the conclusion that he was hiding his relationships with his two baby mamas. Martez responded. "What do you have for me?"

I said. "Some good pussy. You can nut in it and don't have to worry if you got a baby on the way."

"What about Jay?"

"I told you Jay is history." I said.

"I don't feel right feeding another nigga's baby my nut." He said.

"That's what I love about you Martez. You are so crazy. You always make me wet."

Martez asked "How do I make you wet? You was just with that nigga Tank."

"You was just with your baby mama Nikki. So we even."

It didn't take Martez long to get the picture. He knew I would go on and on until I got the response I wanted. When he said he was on his way I rushed into the bathroom and took me a bath. I knew he would not be long since he knew where my new apartment was at. I was caught by surprise when Jay showed up at my door with a diamond ring that he had purchased from Uptown Jewelry off of Bettie Ford Rd. "I'm tired of playing games. I want you to be my wife."

I was shocked that Jay went to the extent of bending down on his knows and asked me to marry him.

I said. "Jay, you must be drunk."

He said "I'm for real Rhonda."

Martez was on his way and here I was with Jay at my door steps, with him proposing to me. I had to think fast to get Jay out the way.

"Jay, I like the ring, but I don't want to marry you. You got a girl." I said.

I knew Jay had apartment across town close to Eastland Mall with his young tender. His cousin Shawn had given me this information when I ran into him at the health department.

"Please Rhonda, I know I'm the daddy of your baby. I wasn't to make everything right." Jay stated.

I could tell the alcohol was talking. This surely wasn't Jay making these statements.

"Jay, you drunk. I don't want you to take this wrong, but I have someone on the way over here." I said.

It was like I put some hot coffee in Jay's mouth. He looked up at me with pain in his eyes. I could tell that he was really hurt when I told him I had company on the way over. "Who is it, Rhonda? Is it that nigga Martez or Tank?" I asked.

Jay was making a scene. I was new to the hood and I didn't know anyone that could help me get Jay away from my apartment before Martez arrived. So, I told Jay to come in. Jay walked inside with his blood shot eyes on me. His Nike outfit looked brand new but his Jordan's were dirty like he had been walking around in a pile of dirt. I offered Jay some milk so he could come down off the alcohol. He declined. I grabbed the phone after Jay took a seat. First, I tried Martez's dope spot number. Then, I tried to beep Martez to give him a heads-up about Jay. He knew my code and called me right back. "Jay is over here." I said.

Martez responded "So, what that got to do with me?"

I didn't think Martez was going to be so nonchalant about Jay interrupting our sex time.

"He's drunk." I said

Martez responded. "Put that nigga out."

It wasn't as easy as Martez was making it sound to put Jay out. Jay was still taking care of me and my daughter. Plus, his sister was till baby sitting whenever I needed her to.

"Martez, you know the situation." I stated.

Martez knew everything I did with Jay. He even met Jays sister after Jay and I had the fight in our first apartment. Martes spoke. "I'm around the corner by the time I get there. Jay better be gone."

This was a new command from Martez. He never demanded or commanded me to do something when it came to Jay. My guess he knew that I didn't care about Jay like I once did.

"Martez. Please wait!" I said.

The phone went dead in my ear. I knew Martez wasn't kidding when he said he was still coming to visit even though Jay was inside my apartment. I rushed to the living room where Jay was sitting on my couch, he had purchased form Rent A Center. He was still in his drunken state.

"Please Jay, leave?" I asked.

Jay responded with a wicked smile.

"Don't make me call the police!"

He spoke. "You don't want to lose your section eight rent money you receive each month."

Jay knew the ins and outs on how I received a section eight voucher from the government. He also knew if I received any violations involving drugs or disputes with a non resident or resident, I could lose my section eight voucher. "Please Jay. Don't do this." I begged.

"I love you, Rhonda." He responded. Then he stood up. I could hear footsteps coming towards the door. I rushed to the door. Then, I looked out the peep hole. It was Jay's cousin Shawn.

CHAPTER 19

MARTEZ

I was one block from Bahamas Apartments at the corner gas station that sat off to the T-shape intersection that ran into Glenwood Dr. My cousin Rico had agreed to meet me at this gas station so he could purchase a couple of hard-boiled eggs. When Rico pulled up, I was hanging up the pay phone out front of the rectangle shape gas station. He hopped out his blue rental Honda Accord after he retrieved his money from his glove box. I pulled the bag from the back seat with the cocaine inside of it. Then, I stepped out my automobile.

"What's up cousin?"

"I got your shit." I said.

The exchange was quick and fast. He tossed the money in the back seat of my car. Then, I gave him the brown paper bag.

"Rico, I need you to go down in Bahamans Apartments with me. I got this situation that need to be dealt with." I said.

My cousin responded. "You know that where I slang my rocks. I probably know the people you talking about."

My cousin was six-foot even, 260 pounds, and he had long braids. His arms were thick like small pieces of logs. He had big thick fingers that had weed marks on the tips from all the weed he had consumed through the day. He was dressed in black Gore-Tech boots, white T shirt, and sweat pants. I could see that he had a lump in the front of his pants. I knew it was a gun. I said. "I need you to ride with me down to Bahamas Apartments."

My cousin responded. "Sure. Anything for you cuzo."

He locked up his car and hopped in my passenger seat. Bahamas Apartments were made up of two-story brick buildings with steel screen doors that protected the wooden light blue doors of most of the apartments. Most of the people that were residents of these apartments were section eight people and low-income people. Rhonda's apartment was a hundred feet away from the the mail boxes. I noticed a gray rental car in front of Rhonda's building when I pulled up in her parking lot. There were a couple of junkies standing around in front of Rhonda's building when me and my cousin stepped out my car with 18' inch chrome rims on it, wrapped in Kumo tires. As we walked up on Rhonda's apartment, my cousin Rico took notice of a hand gun on the floor of the rental car in front of Rhonda's building after he had noticed the Airport Express Rental car's agreement sitting on the seat. He said. "Hold up cuzo."

"What's up?"

"This nigga slipping. He left his gun out in the car."

Rhonda told me Jay carried guns. My instincts told me to try the door to see if it was unlocked. No luck. Rico and I walked slowly towards Rhonda's apartment after Rico raised his shirt to let me know he had a gun. I felt nervous and perplexed about the situation. I had never approached any one over a woman. I rang the doorbell then I stepped back so Rhonda could see me out the peep hole. Rico kept his hand close to his belt by his .45-millimeter hand gun. I knew this 18-year-old would shoot if the situation called for it. He had seen O-Dawg kill in "Menace to Society".

Rhonda opened the door. Her hair was in a ponytail and she was dressed in a T-shirt and sweat pants. She looked afraid. I asked "Are you ok?"

She looked towards the couch in which this light brown skinned dude was sitting on the couch fumbling around with his phone. This guy was to light to be Jay.

Rhonda answered. "I'm fine."

I could tell that something was very wrong inside the apartment, and it was like my instincts kicked in and I could sense the fear inside of Rhonda. "Can you step outside?" I asked.

She said "No."

"Why not" I asked

"I can't."

I watched Rhonda's eyes look towards the door knob of the front door. That was when I noticed a dark-skinned hand holding her shirt. Instantly, I knew this was Jay behind the wooden door. I motioned my cousin Rico with my left hand to come closer to the front step of Rhonda's apartment. He obeyed my command and walked up slowly to me with his hand on the handle of his gun. I motioned to my cousin with my right hand behind my back that someone was behind the door. He stood right next to me after he placed his hand on the trigger of the gun inside his pants. I watched as he aimed the gun towards the door at Jay. My cousin gave me a smile after he touched my shoulder. I said. "I need to use the phone." My beeper was buzzing out of control now. The guy sitting on the couch looked over at Jay. I pretended like I didn't know Jay was behind the door.

Rhonda said. "Just leave Martez."

I watched as Jay squeezed Rhonda's skin in her hip area. She made a unpleasing facial expression to let me know she was in pain from Jay's actions. I pushed the door into Jay and he fell back towards the steps that lead to the upstairs area. Once inside, I smelled old food inside the box shape room that had a brand-new living room suit, TV, photos on the wall and brown carpet throughout the room. Jay stood up after he regained his balance. He gave his cousin Shawn a look like, you gonna help me. I looked over at Shawn to make sure I didn't see a gun after Jay and I had made eye contact. Then I asked "So y'all like to hold women against their will?" They didn't respond.

Rhonda walked up to me but was interrupted by Jay grabbing her by the shirt. The shirt ripped a little. Jay pulled Rhonda closer. Rhonda shouted "Let me go Jay!"

In the blink of a second, Shawn had his gun out. He didn't point the gun at me or my cousin but the gun was now in view. I felt threatened by Shawn's weapon, and it was like I was stuck between saving myself or saving Rhonda. My sixth sense told me to move out of the way so my cousin Rico could have a clear shot at Shawn just in case bullets started flying. I made my way closer to Rhonda as Jay continued to manhandle her in his grip.

Rhonda protested. "Stop Jay!"

Her protest only encouraged him to continue. Jay managed to wrap his hands around Rhonda's thick neck. I watched as Rhonda's eyes stretched like her eyeballs were going to pop out of the sockets, and her breathing became really thin. It was like she was trying to get the leftover oxygen from her lungs. Jay's cousin spoke. "Stop Jay! Let that girl go!"

Jay said "This ain't your business Shawn. Stay out of this."

Rhonda's eyes were directly on me now. She had her hands wrapped around Jay's hands while she was trying to get loose. Jay's cousin spoke. "I didn't come over here with you to get a murder charge. Let her go."

I watched as Jay had loosened his grip. Rhonda's legs touched the floor again and she caught her breath. She stopped coughing after Jay let her neck completely go.

Jay said "I don't have anything against you Martez, but Rhonda is my girl. Imma bout to make her my wife. You see the ring I purchased for her on the glass table?"

I looked over at the small box on the table close to Shawn. There was a ring sitting inside the box with the lid of the box. The ring looked cheap but the diamond gave off a sparkle. I could tell by Jay's speech he was drunk. Rhonda cut in with her protest. "I'm not gonna marry you. I don't want you like that Jay."

Jay said. "That's my baby in your stomach. I don't want my baby to be a bastard because you want to be a whore."

I said. "You see she don't want you Jay. Just let the girl be."

"You Captain-Save-A-Whore?" He asked.

"Man fuck you!"

Jay shot back" Nigga fuck you!"

Before Jay could get all his sentence out his mouth, I rushed him and hit him in the mouth. The punch didn't do much damage because Jay managed to grab me. Then we tussled by the staircase and fell into the doorway of the front door of the apartment. The fight spilled out into the street in which there was already a semi packed crowd waiting outside. I managed to get on top of Jay when we fell to the ground. I spoke. "I'm about to whip your ass for old and new." Then I punched Jay in his mouth, face, head and in his stomach before Shawn pushed me off of Jay. I rolled over to my knees like I had stopped, dropped and rolled in a tornado exercise. It didn't take me but a second to regain my balance and get back on point. Jay rushed over to Shawn after my cousin Rico pulled out his gun. Jay and Shawn tussled over Shawn's gun while I watched the crowd in a panic and then scattered. Shawn finally pushed Jay away and gained control of the gun. I walked slowly toward my cousin Rico who was pointing the gun at Shawn. I spoke. "Don't do it cuz. It's too many people out here."

Rico said. "I need to smoke this fool. He put his hands on you fam. You know I don't play that." The sounds of the police sirens brought me and my cousin back to reality. He put the gun in his pants and we ran to my car. I knew there was only one way in and one way out this hood. There was a 50-50 chance that someone would get my tag number and give it to the police because I had to go pass most of the people that had witnessed the altercation. I pushed my Legend from zero to 60 in 6 seconds flat. There was a blue Chevy truck at the stop sign waiting to enter traffic on Glenwood Dr. when I arrived at the exit and entrance point. I let up on the accelerator as I passed the truck in the right lane. Then I punched the gas pedal once I entered the intersection. We both were breathing heavy from me almost running my car into the back of the truck. I turned into the other lane just in time to enter traffic. Rico and I took in all five police cars racing pass us as we reached Freedom Dr. where he had parked his car in the gas station parking lot.

"That was close." I said.

"I'll hit you later. Go put a car cover over your car. You know this car is gonna be hot." He said.

I put the car in drive once Rico got into his rental care. Then I entered Freedom Dr. and hit the exit to enter Little Rock Rd. I knew if I reached the highway, I was home free.

CHAPTER 20

MARTEZ

I couldn't believe Ty sent Gemini to my dope spot. The guy that I shot outside my dope spot was Gemini right hand man. I found this out from Ty's sister Lady. She had approached me at club Choppers off West Blvd. I was shooting a game of pool with my childhood friend Big Boo, when she had interrupted our game.

"Hello Martez." She had said.

"What are you doing on the Blvd?"

Lady said "Well, I use to live on this side before my brother blew up like the world trade center."

I knew Lady was trying to make conversation. So I played along. I asked "How is your brother Ty?"

"He's doing fine" She had said.

I didn't want to asked too many questions so I asked Lady if she would like to dance. She gave me a proposition "If you buy me a drink. I will give you a dance Martez" Then she smiled.

I purchased a mixed drink for Lady and two shots of gin for

myself. Big Boo couldn't take not being a part of Lady's and my conversation. He had cut in. "Martez, who is this fine ass woman?" Big Boo had asked.

Lady gave Big Boo a smile. She was dressed in a black dress that showed her thick six-foot frame in a revealing fashion. Her heels were three inches high, made by Prada. I did not know the name of her hairdo, but I knew it was the latest fashion that came from the African women off South Blvd.

"My name is Lady" she had said.

Big Boo said "That ain't your real name?"

"That what I go by."

I had cut in "What about that dance?"

Lady and I ate up the dance floor. We did the two-step, and then we did the electric slide. It didn't take long for Big Boo to interrupt Lady and I again. He came with some lame excuse to cut in on our good time. Big Boo had spoken "You got a couple of sales waiting on you outside the club."

I knew what Big Boo was doing. He thought by making me look like a boss, that would help me get Lady in to my bed. I did not want Lady to fall for me just because I was a drug dealer. "Ain't nothing. Shop closed." I had answered.

I had to talk slang and ghetto to Big Boo, because that was the only language he knew.

I continued "Don't answer my beeper no more. Shop is closed. No matter the amount."

Big Boo had taken offense to my comment. He had said "I thought you said business before pleasure." Big Boo had a point. This was something I had always stressed to him whenever I talked business with him. I said "Can't you see I'm handling business with this female?"

Big Boo said "She ain't buying no dope."

I knew Big Boo could be relentless on how to get on my nerves and at the same time make a fool out of himself.

Big Boo reminded me of a brown skinned Biggie Smalls. His

swag was like Biggies but he thought he was in style because that was what Biggie came out rapping about. He even tried to dress like the New York rapper. There were the Timberland boots, blue jeans, and button up shirt. Big Boo even had the same kind of hat Biggie had on in one of his videos. "If you want to serve them, serve them." I said.

I knew Big Boo didn't have the amount my customers were asking for. This made Big Boo drop the subject all together. I had turned my attention back to Lady.

"Do you want another drink?" I asked.

"Yes"

I knew Lady ran with a small circle of female friends that called themselves "The High Maintenance Crew." They were all in the club mingling among other so-called players and bosses. Lady was the ring leader of her crew due to the fact she had been in the dope game since she was a kid. Her brothers had been dealing since they were in their early teens. They were all one year apart in which Ty was the oldest out of Lady's six siblings. Then came Lady, Mark, Curtis, Shawnda, and Lil Dee.

I knew of Lady before I knew Ty because Lady used to hang out with this girl I had a major crush on. In my book, Lady was prestige in the streets, and she was a dope man's dream because she knew the ins and outs of the game. After I had ordered Lady another drink, she had asked, "Do you have a woman?"

The question had caught me off guard. I didn't know how to respond since I was not prepared to tell a lie. I knew I had to be careful how I answered Lady's questions, due to the fact that she was a potential candidate for being my woman. I knew Lady had already did her research on me. This fact was known to me due to the fact of three of her crew members who were from the same hood as me. Keyawn, Tee, and Tasha knew me since I was a puppy. They knew me before my grandmother would let me off the porch.

They had even given Lady all the facts about my life, and

Lady knew about my situation with Nikki. Plus, she knew about Rhonda too. This did not stop me from making my move to put her on my team. I had asked "What do me having a woman have to do with you and me?"

"I don't want to create any land mines in the future. I know how baby mama drama can be."

I didn't know if Lady had any kids. I asked "So, you have been in a relationship with a guy that had kids?"

Lady had laughed. Then she said. "Just say I had my share of spoiled fruit. I hate niggas that lie. It's all about keeping it real."

Lady was showing me what a real woman was supposed to be like. She was asking me to put my hand on the table.

"I can't lie, I've got friends."

Lady had responded. "What about Rhonda and Nikki?"

I knew that Lady had information of my personal life due to Keyawn, Tee and Tasha. They were always inquiring about me through the junkies in the hood. I had said "What do you want to know?"

Lady asked "Do you really have a baby by Nikki?"

"The jury is still out on the situation."

Lady had cracked a smile. I could see she had nice hygiene. Her teeth were pearly white. She had a gold crown on the bottom corner of the front left that gave her a sex appeal. Lady had this old school soul that told you she was up on game. It was like she was looking through my soul as she looked into my eyes with her hazel green eyes. She said "I just like everything to be put on the table. I don't like surprises."

I had to agree with Lady about putting everything on the table. It was best that way.

I said "Do I have to worry about you man?"

She had hesitated then said. "My man is locked up."

I was smiling inside. It was like music to my ears that Lady had a man. I knew this was the green light for me to keep Andrell, Rhonda, and still have Nikki on the side. "I know you don't want to talk about him, but I need to know if I have a chance?"

Lady said "You want to know if you can fuck me?"

"You're so blunt!"

Lady said. "Just say I can read minds. I knew voodoo." Then she gave me a smile.

I didn't know if Lady was playing a joke when she said she knew voodoo, but I couldn't keep myself from asking, "Do you really fuck with that root shit?"

Lady didn't laugh. She gave me this wicked smile that left me in doubt. Then she changed the subject. She said "I heard that you shot Gemini's right hand man."

"Who told you that?"

Lady said "You know that's the word on the streets."

I didn't know the guy I had shot in the back of my dope spot was Gemini's right-hand man. I did not know Gemini had a right hand man. "You know people lie. I don't have any beef with Gemini or your brother."

Lady gave me a stern facial expression. Her eyes became intense along with her muscles in her face. She took a sip of her drink before she said. "I did not hear about the beef between you and my brother."

I was sure Lady was lying. She had seen me come to the rim shop to meet with her brother on several occasions. "You know money make people change." I said.

Lady said "Tell me about it."

Lady and her brother Ty weren't on good terms at the moment, and the main reason they had fallen out was because Lady introduced this guy to her brother and the guy didn't pay for a couple of bricks. The word in the street was the guy was robbed by one of my childhood friends, and on top of that, I was supposed to had put my child hood friend on this guy. I didn't want any beef with Ty. There was too much money to be made to be falling out over turf and loyalty. I felt like I had the freedom to buy from whomever I wanted to. It shouldn't have been a problem even if I made the choice to deal with Nikki's brother Sam. Co-signment wasn't for me. I like being my own boss. I said. "I know your brother want to talked to me. I just don't feel like it's my fault that we went in different directions."

Lady spoke "Word is you put Chuckie up on one of Ty's workers. Chuckie robbed the guy and shot him."

I didn't know that Chuckie shot the guy he had robbed. He told me he went up on Wind Gate, an area that was located about two miles from where I was selling my dope in, and robbed this guy. I didn't want to involve myself in something that I really wasn't involved in so I said. "I don't know about anyone that got robbed and shot."

I could tell Lady knew I was lying. She made another sound with her mouth to let me know that she knew I was lying. "Think," she said, "I fell out with my brother too."

I didn't know if Ty sent Lady to the club to find me. It was hard for me to weed out what motive Lady had, but her motive fell right in my face when my step-brother had walked through the door of the club in a polo outfit like mine. The only thing that was different about our two fits were the colors. He had on red and blue in which made him look smaller than his 5-8 frame. I had on white and blue. Lady's lip dropped like something fell out her mouth. It was like my brother recognized her too and instantly made eye contact with her. I didn't know how they knew each other but the streets of Charlotte were not that big. I asked "You know my brother?"

Lady had broken her stare on my brother, then said. "I used to fuck him." This was new information. In fact, this was good information because my little step brother had this swag that he had taken from me. He was always trying to be the life of the party like me. He also loved the attention from the ladies. "He must be good like big bro!"

Lady laughed. Then she said. "He's alright."

My stepbrother made his way inside the box shaped room

over to the pool table area where I was standing beside Lady then he asked. "Yall know each other?"

"Not like that bro" I said.

My lil brother knew I was quick out the draw. He knew I love women like a fat kid loved cake.

Lady had said. "You didn't tell me Martez was your brother."

Dirty Don wasn't really my blood brother. He and his brother Stacey called me their brother because my mother had a semi relationship with their father. In which my little brother Derrick was brought in to this world out their relationship. This was the reason we called each other brothers. Lady wasn't going to let my lil brother block her plan so she had slipped me her number before she had left the club with her crew. I was puzzled at first, but when I unfolded the pieced of paper with the number on it, I knew she was trying to get a message to me from her brother. The note said: "I can't do what my brother want me to do. You're alright. If you ever want a good time. Just call me." I folded the paper up and put in in my pocket. I did not know I would find out about Ty's plan after my night of fun. Lady had been just one piece of the puzzle. I had a couple more pieces to find.

CHAPTER 21

MARTEZ

I knew Gemini had a tough reputation to live up to. He was running with one of the most notorious drug dealers in the city before the Bloods hit the city. Being Ty's right hand man came with a high cost. Gemini knew this because he had to make an example every now and then just to let people in the city know Ty wasn't to be messed around with. Gemini had served time for a man slaughter charge three years before he had hooked up with Ty. He had known Ty since they were adolescents and they had been selling drugs off and on since their youth. In the street, Ty was known as the brains of the operation and Gemini was known as the muscle. Gemini stood six-foot tall and carried around just under 180 pounds. There was nothing special about his physique but he did have red freckles and his hair was semi red. His skin was light bronze and word was Gemini had a pigment problem with his skin since he had red hair and red freckles. It didn't take Gemini long to retaliate to the incident that happened in the back of my dope spot. There was little time to react to what Gemini had in store for me. I now had Big Boo posted up at my play sisters' apartment. He was doing the night shift now since I was receiving more dope that I could handle from my new plug. Big Boo knew about the beef Ty had against me because I wouldn't deal with Ty and the fact Chuckie had robbed Ty's main block. Word was still echoing in the streets that Gemini was going to take revenge for both incidents. I wasn't into much lip boxing. It was all about show and prove to me. I knew I had violated street law by shooting the guy but the guy had violated by trying to rob my spot. There was a cause and effect to everything I did in my life and this cocaine war was the cause to the black-on-black males committing crimes against one another at the moment. It was crazy because when I was in war, I couldn't see it. When the war was over that was usually when I would realize the true meaning of that war. Some people go into wars for all different kinds of reasons. The reason I was in this war with Ty was three reasons: Reason one, I stopped buying from him. Reason two, I shot the guy in the back. Reason three, Ty believed I sent Chuckie up to his main block to rob his workers. I knew I had to relocate soon, that was why I became involved with this girl named Denise who lived two sections behind my dope spot.

I had a clear view from her bedroom window of my dope spot's back door. This was the perfect spot because I could see all the cars that pulled in the rectangular parking lot behind the building. It was around 2:30 am when I finished pounding Denise's asshole dry. She was exhausted from the two hours of mayhem sex. I decided to go to the kitchen of the apartment in search of something to quench my thirst. When I arrived in the kitchen of the two-bedroom apartment, I noticed a man and a woman walking towards the back door of the apartment. I knew the lady next door smoke crack and she received visitors all hours of the night. I looked closer at the woman as she stepped up on the porch. It surprised me that my aunt Jackie, my mother's sister, was knocking on the door now. She was dressed in a colorful dress with flowers all over it. Her hair was cut short, inches from a small afro. She was two shades lighter than my mother in which she was close to being white. The guy that was standing next to her was a white dude that looked like he could pass for a school teacher. His red framed glasses gave me this assumption. I turned out the porch light as I opened the door. My aunt spoke. "Nephew. Nephew. Nephew. Don't be mad at me. I been drinking." Her breath gave off the scent of white liquor and beer.

I spoke. "Didn't I tell you not to come over here?"

My aunt said "Big Boo down there going in your vial caps. He ain't selling break downs. He selling hand me downs."

I knew how Big Boo operated late night. He was always trying to make extra money for his sex habit. Big Boo was a habitual trick off artist. He always broke down the dope in the vial caps after midnight. This was how he made extra money to support his trick off habit. I asked my aunt how much money this guy planned to spend. She said 150 dollars. Then I asked "Is he the police?"

The guy's blue eyes lit up. It was like the question caught him off guard. He said "No I ain't the police."

"How do I know you ain't the police?" I asked

"Just trust me I'm not."

I said "That's what my people did when they were made into slaves. We trusted y'all white boys and y'all trick us." Then I smiled. I could tell this guy was feeling uncertain about the deal. He turned to my aunt and asked "How can I prove to him I'm not the police?" She said. "Hit a piece in front of him." This was like music to this white guy's ears. I could tell he was a undercover fiend by his demeanor. He tried to keep himself calm, but when I pulled out my rocks his eyes lit up again. My aunt pulled out her glass pipe and I stuffed a rock on top of it. She cooked the rock down on the glass and took blast. Then she passed it to the white guy. He grabbed the glass pipe and took a hit. I knew right then that this guy was either a good actor or a fiend because the way he had responded after hitting the rock. He did like most crack heads. He went silent.

My aunt was an expert. She was past the stage of looking up when she took a hit. It was like she had become more alert when she smoked crack cocaine. I spoke. "Give me the money." My aunt gave me the money. I took it and folded the three bills up and put them in my pocket. Then I gave them instructions to go sit inside the guy's truck. My aunt didn't hesitate. She knew I would bless her with the correct amount of dope as long as she did what I said. I returned to the living room of the apartment and opened the closet door in the box shaped room. There was a blanket laying on top of the nine eggs of crack-cocaine I had put inside the shoe box on the floor. I grabbed the box after I removed the blanket. Then I took out an egg and broke off a pieced that looked close to an eight ball. This was what you call eye-balling crack. This was a special skill I had developed by handling dope over the years. I didn't need a scale to weigh drugs. Just my hands and eyes.

I went to Denise's kitchen cabinet where she kept the sandwich bags and put the crack cocaine inside a bag. I tied a knot in the bag to make my product look pretty for the sell. Then I put up the remainder of the dope. Then I ran upstairs collected my Jordan's and put them on along with a jacket, sweat pants and my fitted nice hat. Then, I headed out the door. After I shut the back door, I glanced out at the large Ford truck that my aunt and the white man was sitting in. I could see my aunt was running the flame from her Bick lighter over the glass pipe. This made me think about checking on Big Boo. I dismissed this thought and locked the door to Denise's apartment. Then, I recognized a red dot on my shoulder of my jacket. I moved slightly to the left as the sound of the gun echoed through the night. Then, I took off running towards my aunt and the white man. There wasn't much light outside in this area. The only lights were porch lights from a couple apartments. I noticed five dudes coming from the opposite end of Denise's building. They were all dressed in black. I couldn't see a face or make out the size of these guys. The only thing on my mind was getting away from the apartment building. The parking lot was 120 yards away now, but I felt like I had broken a track race record when I reached the truck. My aunt was getting out the truck as I had approached it. She started screaming and grabbed my hand as the white guy in the truck pulled away from the curb, blocking the guys from my aunt and me. I heard gun shots as the dudes ran up on the truck. My aunt and I had watched as the guys unloaded on the white man inside the truck. The white guy lost control of the truck and ran into several cars in the small parking lot before the truck flipped over after going over the top of one car like a monster truck. The sound from the truck crushing into the cars didn't put fear into these five unknown men like it did me. It was like my heart skipped several beats. My aunt still had me by my hand as we raced towards my dope spot. I knew the only chance I would have to get away from these guys was make it to my dope spot. I let my aunts hand go as we came across a ditch in which the city of Charlotte Street maintenance had been working on earlier. My aunt fell into the ditch, but I managed to keep my balance. I raced towards the front of my dope spot building after glancing over my shoulder to see if the five men were still in pursuit of me.

I hit the front door like I was trying to knock the paint off the wooden door. Big Boo didn't answer. It didn't take me but a second to decide that Big Boo wasn't going to answer the door. I knew he was either sleep inside the apartment or getting some head from a crack head. I took off running toward the middle section of the hood. In this section, I knew there were other dealers that hung out on Death Row. We call this section Death Row because several people had been killed in this section over the years. When I turned the corner to enter Death Row, there was only one dealer out that I knew had a gun on him. Lil' Nub was sitting out on the porch of his girlfriend's apartment drinking a 40 ounce. He watched as I raced toward him. When I reached him, I said "There are some niggas shooting at me." I was out of breath. Lil Nub was five years older than me, and he stood around 5'2 but he had always carried around a gun that was bigger than his body size. "I really don't fuck with you but you from the hood and these niggas done fucked up by coming to the hood." He said.

Lil' Nub reached under the lawn chair he was sitting in, and he came back up with a semi-automatic weapon. The five guys turned the corner as Lil Nub let off some shots in their direction. It looked like the fourth of July in the projects as the five dudes scattered like roaches.

I cursed myself out because I left my gun at Denise's apartment. Then I went to my grandmothers' crib and waited about a half an hour before I returned to where the white guy was still in the truck. The truck was up-side down. My aunt was standing outside the truck on the driver side talking to the white guy. I walked over and asked "Did you call an ambulance?"

"No," My aunt said.

I did not want to get involved with this white dude, but I knew he knew where Denise's apartment was at and I knew it was a possibility that he could point me out to the police, and also, point out the dope spot.

"You need to call 911," I said to my aunt. I gave her the key to Denise's apartment while I stayed there with the white guy. I had to find out what type of state of mind he was in. I asked "You know where you hit at?" The white guy said. "My whole body is numb."

"Just be still" I said.

The white guy said. "Can I ask you for a favor?"

"Yes, anything"

"Can I get a hit? That was some good shit you gave me," he said then started laughing. I joined in with him.

I was left in a puzzled state after this incident. It was like I was losing control. I didn't know if Jay was responding back to the fight at Rhonda's or Gemini responding for his right-hand man being shot. I came to the conclusion it was Gemini because he had tried to get Ty's sister to set me up. I was right too. It was Gemini.

CHAPTER 22

RHONDA.

Martez's sex game was off the charts in my book of love making. He was number one on my list, surpassing my one-night stand, Tank.

After a session of sweet love making, Martez made several calls in which he told me he had to leave because of business. My alter ego didn't believe Martez so I hopped in my car and I took a trip over to the jungle where Martez had been doing his business. There were a few crack heads standing around the apartment buildings where Martez's dope spot was at. I could tell one was a look out guy and the other two addicts were stuck in their addictions chasing their next high.

They say fiends come in all shapes and sizes. A true statement if you ask me. My action towards Martez was now showing. I was a stalker/sex-fiend and I was no better than the few junkies standing out in front of Martez's dope spot.

I circled the block several times until this crack head named Fast Eddie stopped me on Farmer St. I knew Eddie because he was Martez's barber and main crack customer.

"I'm looking for Martez. Have you seen him?" I asked.

Martez's rental car was nowhere to be found. I was perplexed by this notion due to the fact that he had told me he had to serve a few animals in the jungle. Martez was always spitting that street slang to me and most of the time I understood him due to the fact I was always ear hustling whenever he was on my apartment phone talking business around me.

"By law you know you don't belong around here. You know Martez don't want you out here this late" Fast Eddie said.

"I really need to talk to Martez." I said.

"What's wrong?" Eddie asked.

"Just tell him I came by."

"Why don't you just page him?"

"He is not answering my page." I lied.

Eddie hesitated and spoke. "By law, I don't suppose to tell you this. But I like you."

"What is it Eddie?"

"Martez went to the store."

"What's so wrong about that?" I asked.

"He dosen't like me to tell people where he's at."

Instantly, I knew Eddie was lying. He could not look me directly in my eyes and my sister Tanika had taught me if a man couldn't look you in the eyes than he was either lying or hiding something. My investigative skills kicked in. I wanted to push Eddie some more but my clock on my dashboard showed it was close to 2:00am. So, I decided to end our conversation by telling Eddie "Thanks anyway Eddie."

Most of the street lights in the hood had been shot out. This made it difficult to see up in the dark areas between the L-Shaped buildings. There was over three-thousand people living in these low-income housing projects and there was a high percentage of drugs and alcohol problems inside the hood. I knew I was pushing my luck by exploring this drug infested area but I had been in this hood so many times in a cab that I lost count. I drove to the back area of this neighborhood and pulled in a parking lot where a set of old beat-up cars were parked. I took in the scene like I was an outdoor explorer. There were several large pot holes inside this residential parking lot and a park with two old basketball courts with broken rims. The resident's rental office had a glowing light in the backroom and I recognized a picture of Malcolm X in it. I took in all these details while I explored the area in search of Martez. I rolled down my window and listened to the quiet night. I could hear the buzzing sound from the power lines and the night insects. I noticed a light on at Miss Tiny's crib across the parking lot. Martez had introduced me to Miss Tiny on one occasion after I met him in her parking lot to bring him a box of baking soda. I dismissed the thought of knocking on Tiny's door after I had noticed a man dressed in dark clothes standing on the side of Tiny's building in the mist. Then, I noticed head lights coming in the parking lot behind my car. I quickly moved my car out the way of the oncoming car. Then I reentered the main street in search of Martez again. Once I reached the main street in front of Martez dope spot, I noticed a set of head lights coming down the top of Farmer St. The car stopped in front of Martez's dope spot after passing by me at a slow speed. It was the rental vehicle Martez had been driving all week but Martez was not behind the wheel. What I noticed next sent my heart to my stomach. A bow-legged pecan tan skinned, chick with long hair and slanted eyes stepped out into the lights in front of the car after leaving the door opened to it. I was shocked, and I could not move. It was like fear had taken over my body. My hands, armpits, and the bottom of my feet began to pour with sweat. Several junkies came out of nowhere and assisted this chick with the bags she was carrying. My emotions became mixed by these actions of these fiends because they were treating this chick like she was queen of the jungle.

There were several traits about this chick that stood out to me. It wasn't just her pecan tan skin and her mean walk. This female was several months pregnant. I did not want to jump to a conclusion about this female without first talking with Martez. So, I remained calm and took in more mental notes of this chick. She looked around the same age as me, but she was a few inches shorter and her ass was bigger than mines. When it came to the faces, I blew this chick out the water. Martez slapped this chick on the ass as she entered the apartment. This sent an envious shock wave through my whole body. Martez hadn't ever slapped me on my ass in a playful manner like he did this chick. Yes, I was still in a relationship with Jay but I was only in the relationship with Jay because I felt guilty about him losing his eye. Martez and I had discussed this issue when we first started messing around on a serious level. After Martez closed the door, I found myself lost in my emotions. My eyes were wet with tears the size of lemon drops, and I felt like I had been hit with a softball in the stomach. My whole world had been rocked from under me because I really thought I could have a future with Martez. After using most of the napkins I had stashed din my glove box to clean myself up, I decided to confront Martez and this chick.

I grabbed my pepper spray I had purchased for a cheap price at the Freedom Mall Flee Market and made my way to the front door of Martez's dope spot. Fast Eddie came running up to me right before I reached the front door of Martez dope spot. "By law, what are you doing back here?" He asked.

"You lied Eddie."

"What are you talking about?"

"You said Martez wasn't in that apartment."

"Look here, Rhonda, I don't want to get in between you and Martez's business. I'm just doing what Martez told me to do. That is watch the door and make sure the police don't jump out." He said.

I could see that Eddie had a small glass pipe in his right hand. His book bag that he carried his hair clippers in was laying on the ground a few feet away. He was dressed in a old purple and black Nike sweat suit that looked two sizes too big for his small body. His hair was freshly cut but his face needed to be shaved. "I really need to speak to Martez." I stated as I reached for the door knob. Eddie blocked my path so I could not enter the apartment.

"I cant let you go in there." he said.

"Why Eddie?"

"You know why." He said

Eddie was protecting Martez from me because he knew I was angry by my demeanor. I noticed a police man flashing the huge light towards the numbers on the apartment building. The police man slowly made his ways toward the front of the building after he had noticed Eddie and me. This stupid, nosey policeman was about to spoil my night by interfering with my plan of surprising Martez. Action had to be taken quickly so I headed back towards my car. The cop pulled his vehicle beside my car and stopped. This officer was brown skinned with a bald head with no hair on his face. My opinion, he was an Uncle Tom who was out looking for trouble, since he had a white male partner in his passenger seat. "What's the problem Ma'am?' He asked.

His voice was husky and throaty in which made me feel uncertain about talking with this policeman. "My brother ran off with my rent money." I lied.

"Is that your sibling Miss." The black officer asked as he pointed at Eddie picking up his book bag off the pavement. "No, he ran towards the back of the neighborhood right before you two pulled up."

"What do Fast Eddie have to do with your money?" The officer in the passenger seat asked.

I could tell these two officers were familiar with the area and Fast Eddie. It was time to turn their attention away from Eddie and Martez's dope spot. I put my fake cry together with a few fake tears while the fabricated story I had given the officers was marinating in their heads.

"Calm down miss." The officer said as he exited the car. He was tall, slim and slightly built with a new pressed uniform that looked like he just picked it up from the cleaners. His partner stepped around the car after he had shut the door with a serious facial expression now on his face. "Fast Eddie was trying to help me talk my brother into giving me my money back." I said.

I could tell these two police men had a little doubt about my story because they both could not stop staring at Eddie.

"Get your hands up now!" The white officer shouted at Eddie as he noticed Eddie fumbling around with the book bag. I knew Eddie had a crack pipe in his pocket and some other drug utensils. "He did not do anything." I said

"Be quiet Miss. Let us do our job." The black officer said.

The white officer rushed over to Eddie and detained Eddie with out a problem. I watched as he placed Eddie in handcuffs and put him in the back of the police car. Then, the white officer went through Eddie's book bag.

"Do you have some ID miss?"

"Yes I do." I said.

"Where is it?"

"Its in my car."

"I need to see it." He demanded.

I did not have a problem with these officers doing their jobs but I felt like I was becoming a victim of police brutality when this officer grabbed my ID out my had.

"You don't have to be rude." I said

"Its 2am in the morning, miss, I can be how I want to be. I'm the police. My question to you is what are you doing out here?"

"I told you I'm out here trying to get my rent money back from my brother." I said.

The officer looked me up and down. Then he noticed my diamond ear rings Martez had given me.

"You have nice diamond ear rings on. You sure you ain't no working girl?" the black officer asked.

"You think I'm out here selling my body for money?"

I was dressed in the latest fashion and my hair was done with blond dye on the ends. The officer turned his attention back to my car since I was in a no parking zone. By law, he could have given me a ticket but he decided not to when his partner pulled out small piece of crack out of Eddie's bag.

"Look what we got here." The white officer said. As he held up the small sandwich bag with a small amount of rock in it, the content inside the bag looked like crack to me. I had helped Jay bag up his product on many occasions, so I know how it looked "It's your lucky night Miss." the black officer said. "I'm going to let you go." My heart was relieved when the officer made this comment. I walked slowly to my car after leaving a note on the windshield of Martez's rental car. I was shocked the police did not protest to me leaving the note due to the fact I had fabricated a story about my brother stealing my rent money. I knew Eddie snitched me out, but it did not make a difference. I had seen the girl.

CHAPTER 23

RHONDA

Two Weeks Later

I walked slowly toward the health department building after inspecting my warm up suit and my blue matching Nike Air Maxes. There was a semi crowd inside the lobby area of the building as I signed the checking sheet. I recognized a pecan tan color young woman across the room reading a magazine, and she looked to be around five-foot-three in height with hazel brownish eyes. This female looked like the same female I saw get out of Martez's rental car the night I was looking for Martez.

I decided to approach the chick since I didn't get to say anything to her that night.

"Don't I know you?"

The chick placed the Jet magazine down on the table in front of her then said. "I don't think you do."

This female had her gear together. She had on a cute gap outfit with some sandals that had straps that wrapped around her calves.

"I do know you. I seen you with this guy I know."

The female said. "I'm sorry but I don't really be out in the streets like that."

"I'm not trying to be nosey or funny but you know who your baby daddy is?"

The female shouted "Look here bitch!"

It was like this female's words had knocked the breath out of me. I wasn't use to being called a bitch. Especially in front of a crowd. I said "Who you calling a bitch. You the stupid bitch."

The female said. "No, I'm not the stupid bitch. You are. I know who you are. I seen a picture of you inside Martez's rental car."

"You mean to say my rental car I let him drive."

She said. "Like I said, you the stupid bitch."

The semi crowd turned their attention on this female and me. I could hear some of them saying things under their breaths. I said "I don't want to lip box with you. I came over here to talk to you about situation I have with Martez. We can be women or we can be fools."

The female said "Martez told me all about you."

I hesitated then asked. "Oh, did he?"

"Yes, he said you work for him." She said.

I couldn't let this chick continue to shine like she was the sun so I said in a smart manner. I asked. "Which way?" The crowd gave me an approval like they understand what I was saying. Then this chick went into her ghetto attitude and said "Selling pussy and rocks."

I couldn't believe my ears. This chick was assassinating my character like I wasn't even standing here. I said "He played you like that, trick?"

She said. "What do you mean?"

The female was standing up now. We were about ten feet apart. I said "Martez told me you was just a dirty butt that hold his dope."

"Ha ha ha.. You are so funny. Martez is the father of my baby." She said.

This information was new to me. Martez never told me he had a kid or had a kid on the way.

"So you having Martez baby?" I asked.

The female turned proper on me. She said "Yes. I'm six months pregnant and here for my check up."

There was a few Ah Ah... and some Ooooh ooohhh...

I couldn't let this chick out do me in front of this crowd. So I said "What a coincidence. I'm pregnant too. Martez in my baby daddy."

I gave this chick a fake smile. She didn't appreciate my fake smile because she still responded back with a disrespectful tone. She said. "Look here, I don't have time to be playing games with you."

"I'm not playing games. I'm really pregnant by Martez." Then I poked out my stomach to let her see the evidence.

I knew I was going out on a limb saying that Martez was the father of my child, but this chick was getting the best of me in our lipboxing match. I had to do something to even out the odds.

I really didn't know if Martez was my child's father. It was a strong possibility due to the fact we had sex around the time I think I got pregnant. The two occasions I had sex with Tank made him a suspect too, but I know one of the five Blood gang members could be my child's father too. Jay also was in the equation. I knew I had this chicks' attention now. It was like the proof was in the pudding. She couldn't take her eyes off my stomach. It was like I had cut a piece of this chick soul with the comment. The female came back with the lamest line. She said. "I don't believe it."

"I don't care if you don't believe me. I know what Martez and I did."

She said. "What's your point?"

I stressed "I just want you to know you ain't the only

babymama."

She said. "Child. Please? I know Martez be fucking around. I've heard he supposed to have a baby by this girl named Nikki." I had heard the same thing about Martez, too. It was like this female knew as much as me. To my surprise she wasn't Nikki. I asked "So you ain't Nikki?"

The female said. "What make you think I was her?"

I didn't know anything about what Martez was doing while he wasn't with me. He didn't talk as much after I had given him a key to my apartment. It was like we were just roommates. I asked "What is your name?"

The female hesitated then asked. "I thought you knew my name?"

I really thought this female was Nikki. The night I saw her step out the rental made me mad because Martez and I had just finished having sex. Plus, he said that we were a couple. Martez lied. At the moment there were four reasons I was upset. I was mad because Martez lied to me about not messing around with anyone. Number two. I was confused that this girl wasn't Nikki. Number three. I didn't know who this chick was. Number four. I left Jay for this.

I asked again. "Who are you?"

The female said "My name is Andrell"

The name didn't ring a bell.

I said "Andrell. I don't know you, but I seen you with Martez a couple nights back. He lied to me about you and he lied to you about me."

Andrell said "What do you know about Nikki?"

I didn't want to rain on Martez's cookout, but he violated me by lying to me. I felt like I was entitled to the truth from Martez since he had a key to my crib. I said. "Martez has a daughter on the way and he already has a daughter by Nikki. I know this because my sister got word from a friend and she told me."

I could see the confusion on Andrell's face. She wasn't

believing what I was saying. Martez had lied to her like he did to me.

"Martez told me that little girl ain't his baby. The girl is lying on Martez because he's getting money. I think I know the girl you talking about. Martez used to buy dope from her brother." Andrell said.

I didn't want to put Martez's business all out in the streets so I asked the chick to take a seat. Andrell took a seat next to me.

I asked. "Do you know where this girl live?"

"I don't know where she live. But I know her mother live in Dalton Village projects. I seen her once, but Martez told me not to say anything to her." She said.

I knew Martez had this young chick under his dick spell. It was like everything that came out her mouth had his name in her sentences.

"Have you seen Martez" I asked.

Andrell said "Martez dropped me off."

This caused my emotions to go into a world spin. I had asked Martez to go to a doctor's appointment with me and he almost lost his mind.

"What time he coming back?" I asked.

Andrell said "After he finishes his runs."

I knew Martez was selling dope during the day. We had discussed that he would stop after he had made enough money to get a car detailing business. I said "You don't mind if I wait with you, do you?"

Andrell smiled. Then she asked "You want Martez to fuck both of us up?"

I knew Andrell was new to the streets. The way she had been drilled by Martez had me thinking that he was putting his hands on her when she got out of line. It was like a sense of fear in her voice that made me want to unloosen her chains form Martez. Tears were forming in Andrell's eyes. I could tell her heart was beating fast. It was like the new revelation of Martez being this player made her sick on the stomach. I said. "I just want to get my key back from Martez. I don't want to cause any problems between you two."

"I don't have no beef with you. At first I thought you was trying to play me." She said.

The nurse from the back popped out the door and called Andrell's full name. Andrell cleaned her face and headed towards the nurse. I watched as Andrell disappeared into one of the examination rooms. Then, I got lost in my thoughts. First thing that came to my mind was to call Martez. Then, I thought why not let him come here and see me with Andrell? What would he say when he see Andrell and me together? I thought.

I knew Martez was slick, but this took the cake because he had a baby on the way by this female I didn't know anything about. From the look of the whole picture, Andrell had been doing more than holding his dope. I couldn't stop thinking about what I was going to say to Martez. In my life I had two friends that I thought was alright and Martez was one of them. I didn't take Martez to be a person that played with females' emotions. He had always been a standup guy since the first day we had met. I decided to call my sister Meke and tell her about my situation with Andrell. At the moment it was essential for me to confine in my sister. It was eating me up in the insides to know I had been sucking Martez's dick every day for the last month and a half and he had been sticking his nasty dick in Andrell. Meke answered the phone on the third ring. "Hello?" She asked.

"Meke. I need to tell you something."

I made sure I stressed every word so Meke would understand my issue was serious. "What is it Rhonda?" She asked.

"Martez got this girl pregnant. The little short bitch is here at the health department."

"Which health department? Who Rhonda?" She asked.

"The one on Betties Ford and her name is Andrell"

"What are you doing there?" She asked.

I filled Meek in on my whole situation. Then, I asked her for her opinion.

"You know Martez is my brother. I like him more than Jay. I don't want to say nothing about my brother because I know he got a good reason why he didn't tell you about Andrell." She said.

"That didn't sound right Meke."

My sister knew more about Andrell than I did. It was like everyone know about Andrell and I didn't because when Tori got on the phone she didn't sound surprised.

"Why did Meke give you the phone?" I asked.

Tori said "She got company."

"Everyone knew Martez was fucking this chick but me!"

Tori did not say a word. I now knew the truth. Martez was giving them money not to say anything about his business. I knew money was powerful but I found out that money could make my own family flip on me for the right price. When I called Martez beeper he called back 15 minutes later. "Is this Martez?" I asked.

"Who this?" he said.

"You don't recognize my code? 69?" I asked.

"Look, I have to call you back."

Then the phone went dead in my ear. I knew Meke and Tori had given Martez the heads up on the situation. It was like their loyalty wasn't with Martez it was with his money. The next day both of them had on new outfits and matching shoes. I was hurt, but I learned a valuable lesson. "Money is Power."

CHAPTER 24

MARTEZ

I had found out that Gemini had assembled the crew of gun men that showed up at Denise's apartment building. The type of tactic that Gemini used to get at me was no surprise. I had shot his crew member and would have gotten away with it if Big Boo wouldn't have been running his mouth. We were now in a full-fledged war, and my childhood friend Chuckie was the cause of this war. I knew I would be put in the war due to the fact of Ty's beef with me and my association with Chuckie. The Blood gang members that wanted my turf were also in a war with their rivals, the Crips.

It was like a war zone on the street of the city of Charlotte. It was all over the drug turfs. Rhonda and I were still creeping around even though I advised her that her life would be in jeopardy by hanging around me. She didn't care because she was in love with me. Rhonda had taught me about the two types of love. She had explained that most people weren't in love but they loved someone. I understood exactly what she was saying because I was in love too. Rhonda was wise beyond her years due her early dealings with men. That was where I believed she had learned about the two types of love. When she broke down love, she made it sound like she was teaching a child instead of a young man. I embraced her message about love and put all my relationships that I was having with other women besides Rhonda on Rhonda's love scale. I started out with Nikki first. I gave Nikki a five on a scale of one through ten. I took off points because Nikki wasn't bookish like Andrell. Plus, she wasn't the type of woman I could see as my wife. Nikki had a good side though. She was street smart, good with money, and wise beyond her years. Plus, she was cute, but she lacked the main two traits I was looking for in a woman and that was someone that loved my shitty underwear and bookish.

Now Andrell was clean, bookish, semi street smart, young and loved the ground I walked on. I gave Andrell a 10 because she had all the traits that I was looking for in a woman. The only thing that was now in the way of our relationship was Andrell's drug addict mother. She had found out that Andrell was pregnant after catching me in between Andrell's thick legs. That had been over 6 months ago and now Andrell was staying with her grandmother because she had popped up pregnant after that incident. I didn't hide from the fact I was the father of Andrell's baby. It was my due as a man to embrace my fatherly dues of helping with this child. I wanted to prove to me and the world I could take care of my responsibility, but Andrell's mother had something else planned for Andrell's future. Peggy was Andrell's mother/sister. She had taken Andrell in after she had found out Andrell's real mother had aids. Now Peggy wanted Andrell to join the system like most single parents in the hood. She wanted Andrell to sign up for food stamps and a welfare chick like she was getting for Andrell and Andrell's siblings. I didn't see anything wrong with people getting help, but I didn't want my baby mama waiting in line for a check every month. It was too much to life to be taking the same simple road her mother was taking. I had strong feeling for Rhonda and Andrell. It was like I had taken a pill for love and fell in love with both women instantly. I had love for both women, so when Meke called me and advised me that Rhonda had seen Andrell at the health department on Betties Ford Rd. I had to make a choice. I rushed over to Andrell's grandmothers house after informing Andrell's grandmother I was on my way. When I arrived, I took in the whole hood scenery like a photographer. Andrell's grandmother's neighborhood wasn't a Godly sanctuary. It was drug infested like West Blvd, but instead of apartments these were houses. Andrell's grandmothers house was made up of red brick and old wood. There was a slab of pavement on the side of the house that served as a driveway. There were two large old rocking chairs sitting on the old ranch style porch in which Andrell's grandmother had a blanket sitting on one of the chairs. I knew these were the chairs that Andrell and her grandmother enjoyed during their evening conversations about our coming child. I had met Andrell's grandmother after Andrell's mother put her out of her apartment. This had been 3 months earlier. Miss Betty had embraced me as her grandson instantly. She didn't judge me because I was a drug dealer, and she let me visit Andrell anytime of the day. She also advised me to stay away from Peggy. I took Miss Bettys advice and did what she advised me to do. I stayed away from Peggy. Miss Betty was a large light completed woman, bow-legged, five-foot tall and had long hair that reached just below her shoulder. There was a flaw that matched Andrell's flaw. I now knew where Andrell got her over bite from.

Miss Betty came wobbling out the front door of the house dressed in a blue color house dress as I pulled in the drive way. I could see she had a semi-smile on her face. Andrell joined her on the porch right before I turned off the vehicle. She wasn't smiling at all. I knew she was mad because she had always smiled when she greeted me. Miss Betty had always touched me in some type of way whenever I came to visit. It didn't matter if it was a hug in front of Andrell or grabbing of my hands. I had always responded by telling her how good she looked for her age and how I wanted Andrell to look like her when she reached her age. This had always gotten me points with Miss Betty because she would laugh and be on her way, but this day she didn't laugh. She gave me a disappointing look before she went back into the house. I could hear Andrell's cousin Brad and Tear Bear wrestling inside the house as Miss Betty had opened the front door. I gave Andrell a smile hoping to break the ice between us. She spoke. "I don't see why you smiling." I continued to smile while I took in Andrell's scent and looked over the large T shirt, slippers, and sweat pants she was wearing. She looked over me in the same manner and noticed lip stick on my shirt collar. Andrell spoke "Who the hell you been kissing?"

I didn't understand her notion and the charges she was bringing up against me until I noticed the red lip stick on my polo shirt. I said, "You know how my little sister like to act like she's grown up."

"You think I'm fool Martez?" She asked.

I knew my days of lying to Andrell were coming to an end. This girl was starting to catch on to my games. "I know you ain't no fool. You my girl."

"That ain't what your chick said at the health department today." She said.

I played dumb just to see how much information Andrell had received from Rhonda.

"Stop tripping."

Andrell said "I ain't tripping. You think I'm stupid Martez. I will take you down town."

I knew Andrell was coming into her own, but I didn't know she knew she could take out child support once the baby was born.

"We don't have to put them white folks in our business."

"Well, you need to keep your bitches in check because this

bitch said she's pregnant by you."

I knew Andrell had came in contact with Rhonda from my telephone call with Meke and Tori. It was like I wanted to hear Rhonda's name come out Andrell's mouth to be sure that Rhonda was the woman at the health department that Andrell had came in contact with. So I added gas to the flame.

"You just making this stuff up because you want attention."

"I know you think just because I'm 17 I am stupid, but I want you to know one thing. I know you got that girl Rhonda pregnant. I seen her with my own eyes." She said.

I knew I could be the father of Rhonda's baby, but I also knew I could lose Andrell if I told her the truth. I had lied to Andrell about Nikki. Plus, I had lied about Andrell's semi friend Tee that I was now having sex with.

"Your mind is playing tricks on you. You need to stop listening to that song by the Ghetto Boys."

"I ain't playing with you Martez. I will take out child support and be done with you." She said.

I could tell Andrell was serious because her hazel eyes looked like they were turning fire orange.

"Don't you ever put them white folks in our business. That's the quickest way for me to cut you off." I said.

Andrell just stared at me. She knew I didn't like the threat of putting them white folks in my shit. She knew I was playing dodged ball with the people for my freedom everyday.

"You cut me off you will get what's coming to you." Andrell said.

I knew exactly what Andrell was referring to when she made her comment. The number one mistake I made was asking Andrell to stash cocaine at their grandmother's house. Now this mistake was blowing up in my face. "You can believe what you want to believe. I can't help that these bitches hollering and I can't hear them." I said.

"You have to always be funny, but you better start realizing

I'm holding your dope." She said.

I didn't take Andrell's threat serious but when she turned and walked off, I knew that I was about to lose her. It was something about her demeanor that told me that she wasn't going to tolerate my nonsense.

I blasted the Ghetto Boys song in my sound system before I pulled out Andrell's grandmother's drive way. I wanted Andrell to get the message that her mind was playing tricks on her. Then, I grabbed my cell phone and dialed up Rhonda's number. Rhonda's voice mail came on twice before I finally reached her. It was like she was expecting me to call.

She said. "What do you want Martez?"

"What the fuck did you do today?"

Rhonda let out a small laugh. Then she said. "I told that lil bitch about us."

"It ain't no us no more Rhonda. You know you violated a G-code." I said.

Rhonda asked "So this bitch mean more to you than me?

I was stuck between a rock and a hard place, and my instincts were telling me to be a player and lie, but I didn't want to be looked at as a lying dude to Rhonda. She had taught me the difference between being in love with someone and having love for someone. At the moment I was in love with Andrell due to the fact she was a virgin when I had met her and she was having my baby soon, but I had a very strong care for Rhonda too because I had fought a dude over her and she could also be my baby mama.

"I think it's best we stop seeing each other."

"That bitch must got gold between her legs." I knew Rhonda was dealing in her emotions.

"I just called to say it's over." Then I hung up the phone.

CHAPTER 25

RHONDA

JUNE 1993

Iknew I had crossed the line when I told Andrell that Martez could be my baby daddy too. I wasn't a 100% sure that Martez was the father but I wasn't going to let Andrell make me look like a fool in front of the crowd at the health department so I said Martez was the father. I knew Martez would cut me off because I had disclosed this fact to Andrell. I knew I had a piece of Martez's heart but I knew Andrell had more than I had of his heart. There were several critical facts and rules I had broken by discussing information about Martez to Andrell. The first rule was I broke the player code by approaching Andrell about Martez. Secondly, I told Andrell about Martez's relationship with Nikki. Third, I lied about knowing that Martez was in fact my baby daddy.

I knew it would take Meke and Tori's help to get Martez to talk to me. So I caught a cab over to Parker Heights Apartments off Remount Rd. where Meke was now staying with Tori. When my cab turned inside the small double box shaped neighborhood,

I could see several drug dealers standing in the shadows of the two-story buildings. I paid the cab driver and put my pocket book over my shoulder and walked slowly towards Toris's apartment building. This was a drug infested neighborhood so when I stepped through the door way to enter the first-floor hallway of Tori's building, I could smell a strong scent of urine and crack smoke. There was also a strong smell of old food that was coming from a trash can that was sitting in the middle of the hallway. I walked pass the trash can and knocked on the apartment number two door. Then I looked at my gold nugget watch after I noticed Tori or Meke wasn't coming to the door. It was two pm and the sun was shining bright outside. This was why I was perplexed by Meke and Tori's actions. They were usually up and out, doing God knows what doing this time. "Do you need any help?" A voice echoed from the upstairs area of the building. I looked up to meet eyes with Tori's neighbor Joe Tate. "Have you seen Tori or Meke" I asked. Joe smiled. I had met Joe Tate through Tori when she had first moved into her apartment. He tried to come on to me after Tori left us alone in her living room that same day. I told Joe he was too short for me since he was 5'2 and I was close to 5'8.

"Well, have you seen them?" I asked. Joe walked down the stairs and stood right in front of me and said. "They had a long night, but they are in there." I knocked harder on Tori's apartment door. Joe continued to stare at me. I said. "Why are you staring at me?" Joe said. "I was just looking at how you got into that sweat suit. You look like you are about ten months pregnant."

I knew Joe was picking at me because I had rejected him the last time we came in contact with each other.

"I don't have time for your jokes little boy." I said.

"It look like you got two little boys in your belly big mama."

I began to knock harder on Tori's apartment door until she finally opened the door. "Damn Rhonda, you knocking like you the police." Tori said. She was dressed in booty shorts, t shirt, and bedroom shoes. Her hair was wrapped in a black scarf. Meke joined us at the door. She was dressed in colorful PJ's and her long hair was in a pony tail.

Tori took my pocket book after she threw an old beer can with beer inside the can at Joe Tate. Joe was quick on his feet. He was out the front entrance of the building before the can hit the door. "Why you throw that can at Joe." I asked.

"Because he ain't shit." Tori said.

Joe was a cute, dark-skinned dude that had the beautiful brown eyes. He wasn't my type but I knew Tori had given him some pussy due to their little episode in the hallway. I could smell all kinds of different scents when I entered the two-bedroom apartment, and the scent that stood out was the old fish that they had cooked the night before. My sister and Tori had had a fish fry because they were short on their rent money because they had taken a trip to Atlanta Beach.

"Damn, it smell like somebody's pussy. Y'all ain't on your periods?" I asked. Tori got offended from my comment and said. "I thought the smell was your nasty pregnant ass." I gave Tori a death stare before I said. "It smell like you took too many dicks last night." Tori said. "Do you know who your baby daddy is yet?" Tori statement really touched my emotions. I didn't cry because I had that coming. Meke cut in "Yall know how yall get when yall fall out so yall need to stop before yall fall out." My sister was right about Tori and me. We were always joking on one another and when the jokes went too far, we had always fallen out. I said. "I didn't pop up to joke with you Tori. I came over here because I need you and Meke to get in contact with Martez for me."

Tori said. "Martez dosen't want your pregnant ass."

Meke said "Didn't I say chill out Tori?"

Tori hurt my feelings again, and it was like she was trying to hurt my feelings by reminding me that I was pregnant. "This could be Martez's baby. So, for your information he may want to be with his baby mama after a blood test." I said.

Tori said. "How did you put Martez in your top five?"

Meke interrupted again "Tori, why do you have to be so mean?"

Tori said. "Because your sister is my best friend and we got a love hate relationship."

Tori was right. We had a love hate relationship due to the fact when we were growing up, I had stolen her so-called boyfriend when we were in the 7th grade. I was having sex and she wasn't so I got Joey Dunn from her. At the time Joey was a free agent but Tori liked him. After that incident, Tori and I agreed we would never mess around with the same dude in the future. I said. "Meke don't pay Tori no attention. She just mad because I still got it going on while I'm pregnant." Tori said. "Girl. You two minutes from labor. Don't nobody want your pregnant ass. Especially not Martez."

"You and Meke gonna help me get Martez back?" I asked.

Meke bust out laughing along with Tori. My best friend and my sister were both trying their best not to give me the reality of Martez and my relationship. I knew I messed up when I told Andrell that Martez was my baby daddy. But I didn't know how far Martez would go when it came to dismissing me out his life. It was like he had cut me off like a phone company do when you have an overdue bill. The only notice I had received was that call from Martez to tell me it was over. That was over two months ago. Tori didn't want to call Martez so that left Meke to make the call. I found an old fish plate that Tori had stashed in her refrigerator and I popped it into the microwave. I watched Meke dial Martez's cell phone number, and Martez's voice mail came on. Meke put the apartment phone to my ear so I could hear Martez's voice. I pushed the phone away and told Meke to beep Martez from the apartment phone. We sat there on the white leather couch waiting on Martez to return Meke's call and while we were waiting, we got into my personal life. Tori had a million and one questions for me. The first question caught me off guard because I thought Tori knew me better than she put out.

She asked "Could Tank be the daddy?"

I looked at Tori with a small smirk on my face. She asked again "So is Tank your baby daddy?"

"You can take Tank off the list." I said.

Meke and Tori grabbed their mouths like they were shocked that Tank couldn't be the father. Meke said. "So, who is the father?"

"It ain't one of the five gang members, if that's what yall want to know."

Tori said. "So, it's Jay's baby."

The bell sounded on the microwave gave me an intermission with Tori and Meke. I walked through Tori's small kitchen and opened the door to the small microwave. I fixed me a glass of cold orange soda and returned to the common area of the apartment with my fish plate in one hand and my drink in the other. Tori said. "You need to call you baby daddy and tell him to bring me five dollars for that plate." I had to laugh at Tori's comment myself because I didn't know who my baby's father was. The only evidence that I had that Jay could be the father was the month I had gotten pregnant. I was now eight months. This gave me the notion that it was between Jay or Martez that got me pregnant. I was already a month pregnant before the five blood gang members raped me, so they were erased from the equation. "Tori, I have a joke." Then I took a bite of my fish. Tori took a seat beside me on the new couch she had purchased from Rent-A-Center. Then she said "What's your joke?"

I wanted to tell Tori and Meke how much I like the apartment, but I didn't want my comments to go to their heads so I said. "I don't know which baby daddy to call."

Meke jumped the gun on my comment. She spoke "Don't tell me you been fucking DeWayne too."

I almost choked on my fish. Then I gave Meke an evil stare. I couldn't believe my sister would think I would back track to a guy like DeWayne. "Hell no. I was talking about Jay and Martez."

Tori cut in. "Dam girl. I thought you had lost your mind."

The phone rang and startled all of us. I looked over at the phone like it was a poisonous snake. Meke looked at me before she picked up the receiver. "Hello?" Meke said after putting the phone to her ear. She gave me a smile, and I knew instantly it was Martez. Meke engaged in conversation with Martez for a few minutes before she gave me the phone. I gave her and Tori an evil stare. They read my facial expression correctly before both of them left the room.

"Hi, Martez."

"This you Rhonda?" He asked.

"Yes."

"I told you I was through with you."

I knew Martez was about to hang up on me so I begged "Please Martez don't hang up"

I could hear in Martez's voice that he meant business. "I have been meaning to tell you why I told Andrell you were my baby daddy."

"Why did you do that?"

"Because I was jealous when I saw you with Andrell." I said.

Martez cut me off. He asked. "When did you see me with her?"

"You remember that night you said you had to leave my apartment after you had received a call. I followed you over to Dalton Village Projects. I saw you slap Andrell on her butt. I thought that was Nikki until I ran into Andrell at the health department," I semi lied.

"So, you followed me?" He asked.

I hesitated and said. "Yes, I did. And I'm glad I did because I found out so much I didn't know about you."

Martez got quiet for a full minute. Then he said. "I love Andrell. I think it's best we stop messing around and stop talking to each other."

"You can't just stop loving someone?

Martez said "I don't love you, Rhonda."

"Well, can you do one thing for me then?" I asked.

Martez didn't say a word. I know he could hear my tears falling on the phone. I continued. "Will you take a blood test when my baby is born?"

Martez hesitated before he stated. "I will, just give me the place and time."

"I will after the baby is born." Martez hung up after his statement. My sister and Tori came back into the fully furnished common area of the apartment right after I put the phone down. Meke asked "When did you start begging a man?" I wanted to curse my sister out but I needed her support so I felling in her arms. Then I cried a river.

CHAPTER 26

RHONDA

I couldn't get over the fact that Martez had lied to me. He gave me ear rings as a symbol of his love for me, but I came to find out he was in love with Andrell. I didn't know much about Andrell but I found out her grandmother lived on Tuck Rd after I had done a little investigation of my own. It didn't take me long to get Andrell's grandmothers phone number after I had found out the exact house she stayed in. I dialed 411 and asked the operator for Miss Given's number on Tuck Rd. There was only one Miss Givens listed so I had taken a shot at the number. The first time I called Andrell's grandmother's house her little cousin answered the phone, and I got all the info I was looking from Brad after I told him I was calling from the welfare office. I found out Andrell was now staying there and she was due to have her baby around the same time as me. This gave me the assumption that Martez was having sex with the both of us around the sometime. He had become like DeWayne in my eyes. A liar, a cheat, and a possible dead beat. I was still in my investigative mood when I decided to cruise pass Andrell's grandmother's house in Jay's rental car. Andrell was sitting on her grandmother's front porch dressed in a light blue sweat suit, slippers, and a scarf over her hair when I drove pass. She didn't recognize me because she was too caught up in a conversation with her grandmother. I took a good look at her to see how far along she had come since I had met her at the Health Department.

From the looks of her belly, she was getting big. Her stomach wasn't as big as mine but we were both looking like we could drop the load at any moment. I circled the block a couple of times and then I stopped at a phone booth at the gas station on Tuck Rd. I called Andrell's grandmother's number and waited until someone picked up. My luck Andrell picked up the phone. "You must be really good at sucking Martez's dick bitch!" I said. Andrell said "Fuck you bitch." I couldn't help myself form a laugh. This only made Andrell want to know who I was on the line. Andrell said "If you are a real woman, you will identify yourself." This female had a way with words. She had me wrestling around with my alter ego and she almost got me to feed in and play the game. I remained anonymous and I hung up the phone. Then I smiled to myself. I knew I was inside Andrell's head because she wanted to know who was stalking her. I inserted another coin into the slot of the phone and then dialed her grandmother's number again. This time I hung up when she answered. I did this to get on Andrell's nerves and hope she would have a miscarriage. This may sound hateful, but Martez had broken my heart when he told me he was in love with Andrell. I wanted her to feel my pain and experience the agony I was going through. It was like I couldn't get Martez out my mind. I was constantly thinking about him all the time. There were times in the day I would cry when I replayed the phone conversation when he told me he was in love with Andrell. I had always gotten what I wanted with my body. Especially when I realized how powerful pussy could be. Martez didn't fall under my pussy spell.

My guess he was stronger in the mind than most of the men I had come in contact with. This was one of the reasons I fell in love with him. I didn't know how it felt to be in love with someone that wasn't in love with me until I met Martez. This phase I was now going through was teaching me the different types of degrees of love. Listening to my heart and the voice in my head was telling me I was in love with Martez. There were so many characteristics in Martez's character that made me feel the way I was feeling. All the words in the Webster's Dictionary under charisma described Martez in the most fashionable way. He was alluring, appealing, charming, fascinating, and enchanting. All of these words were him. After I decided not to call Andrell's grandmothers house again, I took a ride to Tuck's rec center to view Andrell's grandmother's house. I was still in harassment mode because Martez wouldn't return my calls. My mind was still on Martez as I drove the long street of Tuck Rd. It was like I couldn't get him out of my system. At first, I had told myself I wouldn't catch feelings for him, but I couldn't control my heart. The only control I thought I had over myself was my heart, and I had let him inside.

As I came up to the intersection where a church and a block of houses formed like a Jesus's cross, I noticed Andrell sitting on the porch with her grandmother. This time, Andrell had the cordless phone in her lap. She looked like she was upset due to the expression she had on her face. Her lips were poked out and she was staring at the phone in her hand like she was waiting on it to ring again. I parked Jay's rental car across the street at the rec center. Then I made my way on to the sidewalk that ran right in front of Andrell's grandmother's crib. There were several people taking walks through the hood no this same side walk. I blended in with the small group of people that were walking along the sidewalk to get a glance at Andrell. I noticed a police car turning on the corner of Tuck Rd. as I reached the front yard of Andrell's grandmother's crib. Then several other cars came out of nowhere. I thought to myself. I'm bust. Then I realized the police wasn't here for me. They were searching Martez's car that he had parked in the back of Andrell's grandmother's house. I disappeared back around the house to the rental. Then I made sure Jay's gun was secured in the glove box before I pulled off.

MARTEZ

Two days later

Rhonda had put something serious on my mind, and she had made me realize I was in love with Andrell. On the other hand, my relationship with Rhonda had been based on lust. At first, I thought it was a bad idea to tell Rhonda the truth, but after talking with Creep about Rhonda, he told me to do what my heart desired. After I expressed the truth to Rhonda, I felt a sense of a cleared heart.

I could hear the wind and the birds singing in Mother Nature, and my mind was sound again. I didn't feel like I was living on two different planets any more. After my conversation with Creep, I had hung up the phone and started thinking about Andrell. I decided it was time to start a new Chapter in my life with her. I was determined that it was time to tell Andrell about my retirement plan, so I called Andrell at her grandmother's house after I made a couple business calls in which I received an order from a business associate. Andrell wasn't thrilled about me coming over and interrupting her evening for some drugs. She was still upset about the police searching my car two days ago. I still made my request. Andrell had already put the four eggs of cocaine inside a plastic bag, and when I arrived, she picked up the bag off the living room table and held it in front of her fat belly. Then she said. "I'm tired of you using me Martez."

"Don't start with me Andrell."

Andrell's grandmother and her two younger cousins were gone to social service for a well-check visit. Andrell decided not to go because I asked her to stay so I could talk to her and pick up my drugs.

She was upset and mad because she had taken all morning dressing herself in a gap outfit and now, she wasn't going anywhere. My timing with Andrell had been off since she had gotten pregnant. It was like I was always showing up at the wrong times. She said. "You think I'm supposed to jump every time you say jump. Ever since I got pregnant, you have been treating me like shit. You don't spend no time with me. It's like you are a shamed of me."

Andrell was right in a sense. I hadn't been spending time with her. Her being pregnant wasn't the reason I wasn't spending time with her. At the moment, I had too much on my plate. I was getting my detailing car business started and I was trying to get my night club off the ground. Andrell didn't understand I was doing so much for our future. All the money I was making was going towards all my business ventures and our dream home. My main goal was to get out the drug game with some money. I thought it was best to keep Andrell in the blind until I was finished with every project. "I'm not ashamed of you Andrell. It's just that I'm trying to make a better life for the both of us." I said.

"I can't tell, you don't tell me anything and the only time you call is when you bringin some dope over here or picking it up."

"Just give me my bag." I said.

I made an attempt to take the bag out of Andrell's hands. She positioned her fat belly in my path again. I pushed her a little bit to try to grab the bag. Her belly bumped the glass table. I could see the shock in Andrell's eyes. She said. "This shit right here means more to you than me?"

"No." I said.

"I should have given this shit to the police the day they searched your car." She said.

At the moment anyone would have thought I was a drug addict from my actions I had displayed.

"Give me my shit." I said then made an attempt to grab my shit. Andrell said. "This shit really does mean more to you than me?" I made another attempt to grab it. Andrell blocked this attempt by turning her back against me and pushing her butt against me. I didn't get any affection from her actions, because all I wanted was to get my shit and leave Andrell. Andrell made a sudden move and managed to get out my grip. She ran out the front door after tossing her shoes to the side. I ran out the door behind her because she had the bag of drugs in her hand. Andrell ran around my car to put the car in between us. Then she said. "This dope really means more to you than me and my baby." I didn't respond in the manner Andrell thought I would. Instead, I just gave her a stare that could spear the soul of a human being.

"You can't talk now Martez?" she asked.

Silence, nothing, zero, I didn't say anything.

"I tell you what. Since this shit mean more to you than your kid and me, get it out the street."

Andrell threw the bag of cocaine out in the middle of Tuck Rd. I was lucky that there wasn't much traffic in the hood because my bag of drugs could have been run over by a car. I got my drugs out the road then I made my way to my car. Andrell was standing in front of the car breathing heavy and looking like someone had painted her skin light red. I was disappointed in Andrell's actions, because she had never acted so immature around me. Her actions were telling me that it might be a mistake to make her my wife but my heart was seeing the virgin I had met several months ago.

I turned the ignition to the motor of my car. Andrell still didn't move. She shouted "Run me over!"

There was no way I couldn't get out the drive way without running Andrell over. I had backed up in Andrell's grandmother's drive way to have easy access to the main road. Now that access didn't exist due to Andrell standing in the way. I shouted "Get out the way!"

Andrell said "Not until you tell me if you gonna be with that bitch Rhonda or me."

I was shocked that Andrell was bringing up Rhonda. The little episode they had at the health department had been over two months ago. "You know I want you. So why the hell you tripping?" Andrell answered, "That trick been calling my grandmother's house. I don't know how she got the number but you need to check that bitch." I didn't have any idea how Rhonda had gotten Andrell's grandmother's number. I was perplexed as her.

I managed to talk Andrell into moving out my way. Then, I decided I would end this beef between Rhonda and me. I called Rhonda at her apartment. No answer. But I left her a threatening voicemail.

CHAPTER 27

MARTEZ

After I called and left some more threatening messages on Rhonda's voicemail, I placed a call to Nikki. I decided to put Nikki on my team after I found out she had a friend with a dope spot on Belmont St. It was in the heart of North Charlotte. This was a drug infested area where Nikki's brother Sam had on lock before his arrest. This friend of Nikki's had been in a relationship with Sam and now had all Sam's clientele coming to her house. The house wasn't nothing special. It was a three-bedroom home. Nikki took over the house so she could help out with her brother's lawyers and bond money. She was truly a soldier in my book. I decided to seize the moment by taking over the spot by putting some crack cocaine in Nikki's hands. She was on co-signment. I gave her two days to get rid of a couple ounces. After a couple of rounds of moving small weight, I moved Nikki up to four eggs. Things were cool until I had found a picture of Keosha on the windshield of my car. I was parked at Double D's Night club right off Wood Lawn

Rd. close to the McDonalds, when I picked the photo up. It was small, but big enough for me to recognize it on the windshield.

My sixth sense kicked in. I knew it had to be Nikki who left the photo or someone that Nikki knew. Nikki didn't sound like she wasn't in the mood for answering any questions but I still asked her about the picture.

"I don't know what the hell you are talking about. I didn't put the picture on your windshield." She said.

"Who the hell you give Keosha picture to?" I asked.

"Willie dosen't have any pictures of her that I know of," she said.

I could hear how perplexed Nikki was about this situation. She was just as confused and in a frenzy as I was. She had no idea who could have gotten a picture of Keosha besides Willie. Plus, she was still asleep. It didn't shock me when Nikki hung up the phone in my ear. After she hung up, I looked at the time on my watch. It read seven am. I had to laugh at myself because I was overreacting about this picture. There was too much on my plate to be wreaking havoc about a picture of my daughter. I was calling Keosha my daughter now since Nikki was making me money. The jury was still out on Keosha even though she had a birthmark like mine on her face. The reason the jury was still out because I found out Nikki was messing around with a dude I had grown up with named Shawn. He was from Dalton Village Projects too. The reason I was cautioned about claiming Keosha as my daughter even though the evidence was strong was because I had seen too many men jump to claim a child and came to find out the child wasn't their child. This type of hoodwink was going on every day in the projects and I didn't want to be another statistic. That was why I was cautious.

I dismissed my thoughts about Nikki and Keosha. Then I headed to my spare room in my two-bedroom apartment. I grabbed my safe from under a stack of clothes inside the closet. Then I walked back inside the common area. I didn't like to bring

Andrell to this apartment because I kept the money here. I didn't want to put her and my unborn child in harm's way so I talked Andrell into staying with her grandmother until I could find our dream house. I now had the 10,000 dollars for the down payment for our four-bedroom home. It was now Monday morning and close to opening time for the real estate office to open. I had an hour before I was due to meet with Mr. Johnson. I put the ten stacks inside a brown paper bag after wrapping rubber bands around the money. Then I took a shit, shaved and showered. Then, I put on slacks, white dress shirt, and a pair of black gators. It didn't take me long to get myself in business man shape. I called Mr. Chad Johnson before I hopped inside my 929 Mazda. He told me he had the keys to my home and the paperwork ready for me to sign. Then he said to meet him at my new house. I decided not to call Andrell because I wanted her to be surprised when I gave her the keys. Plus, I had this crazy feeling in my gut that something was gonna get in the way of my future. I arrived at my new house at 9:00am. The house was close to Carolwinds Blvd right on the state lines of North Carolina and South Carolina. I decided on this place after I spent some time at my cousin's spot in Pageland, South Carolina. Mr. Johnson was dressed in a blue pin striped suit with a pair of crushed blue gators, and he had hair that looked like ocean waves. Standing at six feet tall and built up like someone took a chisel and chipped him the perfect body, Mr. Johnson was what I called eye candy. Mr. Johnson's light skin and his kiss ass demeanor gave me the perception that he could be an Uncle Tom when I had first met him. But Chad turned out to be a blessing because he could get stuff done if I had the cash and if he couldn't get it done, he could point me in the right direction. I gave Mr. Johnson the cash before I had to sign some more papers in which he instructed me that I would have to pay 2,500 dollars a month due to the fact I couldn't get approval for a bank loan. I agreed to rent to own this house in which Mr. Johnson got the owner to go along with this ideal. The asking price for the house was 175,000 dollars Mr. Johnson got the guy to sell for 150,000 dollars on condition that I pay the house off in a five-year period. I agreed to the contract even though I thought 2,500 dollar a month was a lot of money for this home. Plus, the under the table interests. After getting copies of my paperwork and turning the money over to Mr. Johnson, I accepted the keys. I took another tour of the home before I walked back out to my car. Reality set in as I looked to the sky to thank God. I knew this might sound crazy but growing up I was raised by a God-fearing grandmother. So, I took on believing in God too.

My phone interrupted my praying session. I answered the phone on the second ring. I didn't recognize the voice on the line but this person knew Nikki.

"Where is Nikki?"

"The police took her. They said something about the FEDS need to talk to her." The voice said.

I damn near panicked when I heard that the FEDS wanted to talk to Nikki. This sent a shock wave through my body. I didn't know why they would want to talk to Nikki. She hadn't been in business with her brothers.

I asked "How long has she been gone and who is this?"

The voice said. "Right after she got off the phone with you this morning. This her cousin Tiff."

I ended the phone call with Tiff. Then I drove over to Little Rock apartments where Big Boo was waiting on me. He was sitting on his front porch dressed in jeans, Air Force Ones, T shirt and a do rag on his head. There were a couple of crackheads out, running down cars on the block. I stepped out the car and walked over to Big Boo. He started smiling from ear to ear when he recognized the package in my hand. "What's up Martez?"

"I got that work for you" I stated. I gave Big Boo his package. Then, he tossed me the money he had wrapped in brown rubber bands. I had talk to Big Boo the night before. He had told me to come to his spot after I took care of my business with Mr.

Johnson. Big Boo was always ready. That was what I like about him. I asked "Have anyone got busted in the last 24 hours that you know about?" Big Boo eyes lit up. Then he stated "Yes, there was a bust over on Belmont St. in North Charlotte this morning. They say a couple of females were picked up by some city police." I looked at my watch. It was now 12pm. I knew Big Boo was talking about Nikki's spot. Tiff had told this story, too. I took the information that Big Boo gave me and decided to call Nikki's cell phone. There was no answer. This left me perplexed and I had more questions. Would Nikki set me up for her brothers? Would she tell the police I have been giving her drugs to sell?

I dismissed these questions. Then I decided it was really time to exit the game. I called Andrell to let her know I was on my way to pick her up. Her grandmother answered and said "She ain't here." I dismissed Andrell's grandmother's motion before I answered my other line. It was Det. Baily. I had decided to answer the phone because I wanted to know how Det. Baily got my number again. He said. "Martez, why you keep dodging my calls?"

"I don't have anything to say."

Det. Baily said. "It's been about a year since Val was shot, but I think I'm on the guys that shot her. A little help from you will help my case."

I interrupted Det Baily "You can't get no help from me. I'm not a police officer."

"It's about doing the right thing." He said.

"I already don't the right thing." I said.

Det Baily paused before he stated "I know what you did to that guy in the back of your dope spot. I know you shot him." I didn't want to get into a trial on the phone with Det Baily. Instead, I said. "I don't know what you talking about."

"I think you know and a jury will find you guilty of assault with a deadly weapon." He said.

I still don't know what you talking about." I said.

"I know Val isn't your sister too." I wanted to hang up the phone but I continued to listen. He said. "The Feds are watching you. They know more than you think they know."

"Then why haven't they indicted me yet?"

Det Baily said, "In due time. Trust me, you will go down."

I hung up the phone on Det Baily. Then I called the cell phone place and told them I would be there to change my number. After going over the cell phone store on Clanto Rd. and getting my number changed, I called Andrell's grandmother's house again. She told me Andrell had headed over to Dalto Village Projects to visit her mother. I knew Andrell and her mother wasn't on good terms due to the fact she didn't like to be around her mother when her mother was drinking alcohol. The two were like day and night. When Andrell's mother was intoxicated, she acted like a wild woman. I had witnessed Andrell disapproval of her mother's behavior whenever her mother was intoxicated. I decided to drive over to the Dalton Village since I had to check on my play sister. She had been selling small amounts of drugs for me ever since I changed location. I was dropping her packages off every two to three days.

My play sister, Lorna, was standing in the front door of her apartment when I pulled on the front street. Farmer St. was live. There were crowds of people standing out like a big event was about to take place. I looked at my watch. It was one pm. Then I thought to myself, the vice squad must have hit a spot. I walked up on Lorna on the front step and gave her a hug. She couldn't get the words out her mouth fast enough. Lorna said. "Andrell pulled a gun out on Tee and Tee called the police and now Tee is threatening to take out a warrant."

Tee was this light skinned, slim built, pretty little female that stayed in the back hole of the projects. I took Tee out to dinner and purchased her a pair of Nike Air Maxes in the past. It wasn't anything serious. Then, I took her to the Motel 6 and you know the end of that story. Somehow, Andrell found out about my infidelities. She approached Tee and pulled out the chrome .22 pistol that I gave to her. I was relieved to hear Andrell didn't shoot Tee or they didn't get into a fight. Lorna had filled me in on the details since she had witnessed the whole scene. I hit her off with some more drugs before I called Andrell and cursed her out. I gave her an ear full before I hung up the phone. I knew my name was going to get hot and this incident would get to the police. Instead of running from the incident, I approached it head on. I called Tee and met with her again. I took her to the Courtyard Hotel, and fucked her brains out. Case closed.

CHAPTER 28

RHONDA

The first voice on my voicemail was Det Baily. I knew he was still investigating Jay's case, but I still didn't want to be his witness. Then came a female. I knew it was one of Jay's little tenders he was hanging out with. Fighting on the phone with females over Jay had become an everyday routine for me. My mechanically performed procedures I had perform every day in response to these females was to hit *69 and let them have a piece of my mind. Today it was Martez. I could hear the anger in his voice on my voicemail. Yes, I had violated by calling Andrell's grandmother's house but I felt like I was entitled to know why he impregnated this female? What did she have that I didn't?

After calling Martez back and breathing heavy over the phone line, I walked back in the bedroom where Jay was asleep. I slid back under the covers in the waterbed Jay had purchased for himself for his 25th birthday. Then, a pain hit me so hard I thought I was about to die. Then came this wet feeling in between my legs. It felt like someone had poured water in between my legs. I reached for the phone on the night stand. Jay had the phone stationed on the other side of the bed. Before I could reach it and dial 911, Jay was up out of his coma.

"What's wrong?" Jay asked. He could tell by my demeanor I was in major pain. Jay grabbed me by my arm and helped me out the bed after taking the phone out my hand. Then, he advised the operator on line to send help. I could hear the operator instructing Jay to make sure I was in a comfortable position before Jay got off the line. He did just what the operator ordered. He walked me to the living room and made sure I was in order when the ambulance arrived. My hair was all over my head, and I was dressed in a polo house coat, t shirt, sweat pants, and bedroom shoes. At the moment I didn't care about my appearance. I was in so much pain that I wanted my daughter out of me. She had been kicking all damn day. Three months before, I had gotten an ultrasound done, and I knew this baby inside my stomach was a girl, but I still didn't know if Jay or Martez was the father. At the moment, I didn't care because the pain was unbearable. Jay wiped my tears away. Then, he rubbed on my belly hoping this would ease the pain. I was upset with Jay because he decided not to rent a car for the weekend. Usually, he would rent a car. Finally, the ambulance arrived. I don't remember much before Kema light skinned body popping out my tail, but I do remember Jay was standing right their cutting the cord. I decided on the name Kema right after the doctor gave her to me. Kema had the most beautiful brown eyes that reminded me of Martez's eyes. Then I noticed her ears, they looked like they could be a trait from Jay. At the moment, I felt happy, relieved, and confused all bottled up in one.

I started crying when Jay asked to hold her again. It was his way of bonding with his daughter in which I knew he would be a good father even though Kema wasn't his blood child. I called Meke and Tori. They came up to my room after Jay left. Meke walked in looking like the same old hoochie mama. She had on a tight body suit, heels, and her hair was done up in African braids. Tori on the other hand had on a sweat suit with rollers in her head. She said "Where are both of your baby daddies?" I knew Tori was trying to be funny, but Meke took offense. Meke said "Now ain't the time Tori." Tori continued. "Do we have to sign up for Maury or Jerry Springer?" I gave Tori an evil look. Then I rolled my eyes at her. She rolled her eyes back. Meke was watching Kema as the nurse entered the room with Kema in her arms. I could see the shock inside my sister's face. At that moment, I knew she was looking to see who the baby resembled.

"Who do she look like?" Tori asked.

"Not like you. Girl-man." Meke said.

I had to laugh at my sister's comment. It had been a while since Meke made a joke about Tori's problem with hair growing above her lips. Most of the time, Tori would shave before coming out in public, but on this occasion, she had rushed without shaving. This comment by my sister ended Tory and my feud. Tori was now upset with Meke because she didn't like no one and I mean no one to comment on her lip hair. This was a super sensitive subject for Tori. I cut in "Jay is the father." Meke asked "So Jay took the blood test and he's the father?"

I had been in labor for ten hours and ten minutes and now I was being put through another interrogation. It was like my sister and Tori had the same outlook that Det Bailey had. It was like they could look in my tired eyes and see that I knew the truth but I wasn't revealing it. I didn't want or plan to lie to my sister and my best friend, but I didn't want to be their punching bag for jokes either. So, I told them Jay took the test and 99.9% Kema was his. Plus, I told them that Jay signed the birth certificate. Tory said "Damn! Damn!"

Meke started laughing and then said. "Don't be cursing around my niece." I didn't understand why Tori was so upset until Meke said. "Tori. I want my hundred dollars." I couldn't believe my sister and my best friend had placed a bet on who was the father of my child. I was upset with both of them. I couldn't believe they were acting so immature. I said "Meke, you know better to bet on my pussy. This is my pussy and I can do what I want with it."

Meke started that stupid little laugh she knew I hated to hear. I said "I don't see anything funny. You better be glad I just dropped this baby." Meke and I had had our share of fights. Most of the fights I had gotten the best of my sister until our sister Tanika started helping Meke out. Then, it would end when my mother would come in with a belt and beat all of us. Tori and Meke stayed for another two hours before they left. I was now alone with Kema. My emotions started running wild when I started thinking about my current situation. I was now holding information inside that I would have to take to my grave. I knew Tori wouldn't let this blood test situation go without seeing a test for herself. She had lost a hundred dollars to Meke and Meke was rubbing it in her face and to spice things up I didn't know how Martez would act when he saw Kema. I decided to call Martez at his dope spot to let him know I had Kema. He answered the phone on the third ring. I said. "Martez. This is Rhonda."

"What do you want?" He asked.

"I had the baby." There was a pause over the line. Then he asked. "Is it a boy or a girl?"

I was surprised he asked because I knew he was in love with Andrell and he let it be known she was a virgin when he had met her. I said. "It's a girl." The line went silent again. I could picture Martez making a serious facial expression the way he did when he was thinking. I knew at this very moment he was thinking, so I asked "Martez, are you still there?"

"I'm here?"

I said. "You don't have to take the blood test."

Martez responded. "I'm not playing no games with you. Imma take the test."

"Martez, I don't need you for anything. I think it's best that you don't be a part of Kema's life."

"I guess it is Mama's Baby Daddy's Maybe."

"What do that supposed to mean?" I asked.

"You know what it means."

"If you wouldn't be so childish maybe we could work something out." I said.

Martez interrupted. "Wait a minute. You are the one who like to play games. Following people around spying on them like you are married to them."

I cut in "I wouldn't never marry someone like you. You too selfish Martez. You only think about yourself."

Martez responded "Look who's talking. You ain't Miss Perfect. You know you was fucking me and Jay at the same damn time. Who's the whore?"

"Your mother is a whore. That who's the whore!" I shouted into the phone.

I knew I had violated when I called Martez's mother a whore. There was a thin line between love and hate and I knew how much Martez loved his mother so I only said it because I knew this would hurt his feelings.

Martez said. "You know you ain't shit in my book. You will never be shit. Look at your mother and your drug addict father. That's why you are fucked up the way you are."

Martez's words were like a knife cutting into my soul. They say words don't hurt the soul but that's a lie. My feelings were burning with the juice of revenge. Martez had hit a nerve. He was showing me that I would have to be a mother to my child no matter what stood in my way. Martez knew how much I loved my parents. Even though I grew up in a dysfunctional setting where my mother drank and my father used crack cocaine, I still managed to love them. They had still taught me the meanings of love and how to still love them no matter what.

I had to defend my parents so I said "Martez, you know how much I have been through with my family problems. You know how I was molested as a kid and what I went through after my molestation and you have the nerve to talk shit about my parents.?"

"Ain't no limit in war. You always have taken my kindness for a weakness. You tried to break up Andrell and my relationship." I cut in "I don't want you Martez."

"It's the other way around. I never wanted you for my girlfriend. I just wanted to have sex with you. There, now that's the truth." He said.

Martez was an expert at hurting my feelings. He knew he had the key to my heart and also the power over me that I didn't know he had over me until I realized Kema was his daughter. Thinking about his seed growing inside my belly had only made me depressed while I was carrying Kema. I knew the whole time Martez was the father but I had this little hope that Jay could be the father. I knew Jay was better fit for the position. Martez was too much of a player to be a father. His player tactics gave him power over me. He knew how to say and do the right things to put me under his spell. That was why I said Martez was an expert at hurting my feelings.

"I knew you just wanted to have sex and I also knew you was in love with Andrell because you hid her from me. The day you gave me them ear rings, I knew you was dealing with your lust." I said.

He said. "Ok, you got me. I was thinking with my dick. I let my little head take over my big head."

"See Martez, it's always a joke with you. That's why I called to asked you to keep this between us."

"What are you saying Rhonda?" He asked.

I paused my breathing for a few seconds before I stated "I know you are the father."

"How do you know?"

"Jay took a test. It ain't his Martez."

"How do you know it's mine?" he asked.

"My cycle and we had sex without a condom."

Martez still wanted a blood test. He didn't believe a word I said. I was good when it came to lying and keeping secrets. After going through being molested by my mother's boyfriend and selling myself for money through the years, it was time I grew up and changed. I knew I couldn't change Martez's mind about the way he felt about me but I knew I could change my ways and then maybe we could work on us for the sake of Kema. Martez agreed to keep this secret between us. I knew he was only doing this because he was trying to keep his union with Andrell. Kema was evidence against Martez, and if Andrell knew Kema was in fact his daughter and I was the mother, this would have broken Andrell's pure heart. I knew Andrell was in love with Martez. My guess Andrell was in love and her love for him was blind.

The next day…

I was lying awake feeding Kema in the living room of my apartment when my apartment phone began to ring. I looked over at the small clock on my common area wall before I answered the phone. Breathing heavy on the other end was Tori. Tori shouted "He's dead Rhonda. He's dead." The word dead instantly made me want to know who Tori was talking about. I said. "Calm down Tori." I could hear Tori catching her breath. Plus, I could hear traffic in the background. I continued. "Now tell me who's dead?"

Tore shouted "Tank!" Tank's named sounded off in Tori's voice. I went numb instantly. It was like my nerves in my body had stopped working. Tori said. "Rhonda are you there." I couldn't hold back my tears. Tears fell off my cheeks on to my daughter Kema. I said. "I'm here." Then I asked "Who did it?"

Tori hesitated and said. "He shot a couple blood gang members before he was shot on the Blvd."

"How many Tori?" I asked.

"Two and he wounded three bitch!"

I knew this was Tank's way of retaliation for me. I said "Where are you?"

"I'm at the Waffle House on Clanton Rd."

"Where is Meke" I asked.

I could hear a couple of voices in the background as Tori reached Meke the phone. Meke said "Rhonda, its crazy out here. Everybody that was at the club are out here. I mean everyone." I could hear in Meke's voice that she had seen the incident between Tank and the Bloods. Her tone gave me this assumption when I asked. "Meke, did you see Tank get shot?"

"Yes Rhonda. It was sad." My sister started crying. I said. "Meke, I need you and Tori to come to my apartment."

Meke agreed that her and Tori would come right over after they had received their food they ordered. I hung up the phone and then changed Kema's pamper. Then I walked to the kitchen and got the half of bottle of gin that Jay had left at my apartment. I putted me a glass of gin and lit up the half of blunt of weed that Jay had left in the living room in the ash tray. An hour later Meke and Tori walked in with their boxes of food in their hands. Meke's eyes were bloodshot red and Tori's make up was smeared around her eyes. I knew they both had seen Tank killed and this was why they were suffering at the moment. I looked over at the clock in the living room, and it was now one am. I hadn't heard from Jay since midnight after he hung up on me at his little spot in North Charlotte. He had told me he was going to Club Chopper before he ended our conversation. I knew he knew about my little episode with Tank. Jay had said "I just called to tell you, your little boyfriend got killed."

I could hear in Jays voice that he had been drinking. I played dumb "What are you talking about Jay?" Jay said "You know damn well what I'm talking about"

I had decided it was best not to get in to it with Jay because he was doing too much for me at the moment.

Jay had expressed his feelings about Tank before I had ended the call. I had told Jay that I had never been in love with Tank but I did care that he was dead, if he was in fact dead. I knew this truth would piss Jay off and I knew this would give me an exit to hang up on his drunk ass. I turned my attention towards Tori and Meke.. "Yall have to tell me the whole story. I don't want yall to leave a word out." I said.

Meke asked "Why are you drinking Rhonda?" My sister knew I only drank on special occasions.

"I have so much going on with my life. I'm stressed." Meke didn't know that Martez and I were still at war. She didn't know Martez was Kema's daddy. All of the pressure of keeping my relationship with Jay and keeping the fact that Kema was in fact Martez's daughter was taking a toll on me. Plus, Tank's death added to the stress because he was killed trying to protect my honor. I decided I would tell Meke and Tori that Martez was in fact Kema's father so I could get some of the stress I was carrying around out. I said. "I know the subject should be on Tank but I have a problem that's been stressing me out and that's why I been drinking."

"So, you have been drinking other than tonight?" Meke asked. "Yes."

I wanted to tell Meke and Tori about what Tank promised to me. I decided to keep this secret for my new diary. Instead, I told them that Martez was in fact Kema's father. Tori said. "Where the hell is my hundred dollars Meke?" I couldn't believe my best friend and my sister would start fighting over a hundred dollars knowing I was in a time of stressing. They got into a little lip boxing match. Meke said "Rhonda, you know you said at the hospital that Jay was the father"

"I did but the blood test I received in the mail said it wasn't Jay's baby."

Tori said. "That leaves Martez as the father."

My sister wasn't trying to pay the money back to Tori so she said. "Martez might not be the father either." I knew my sister was calling me a whore, but I didn't want to fall out with her at the moment. At the moment, I need her. So I said. "Martez is the father. Like I said. I know who my baby daddy is." Meke said. "Martez didn't take a test."

I didn't want to get into a debate with Meke so I left her and Tori inside the common area of my apartment. Then I went in got inside my bed with Kema after I had checked on Sherie, my oldest daughter.

Next morning…

Morning came quick. It was like I didn't get any sleep. Kema woke me up with her cry because her pamper was wet. This was something she did every morning to get me out of bed. Other than that, she was a good baby. I changed Kema pamper and made her a bottle. Then I walked back inside the living room where Tori and Meke were asleep on the floor. They both looked like they had had a long night. I knew they did but I had a lot of problems I had to deal with that was on my mind. So, I woke them up. "Meke, Tori!" They both turned over. I said. "I want to go to Tank's funeral." They agreed they would go with me if I let them go back to sleep. Meke had made a smart comment about me paying Tori the hundred dollars because of my big mouth. Then she said. "I will go if you pay the hundred." I knew Meke was serious, so I agreed to pay the hundred.

A week later we attended Tank's funeral. It was a packed house being that most of the North Charlotte hood knew him from riding his motorcycle in the hood. But it was a closed casket when it came to Tank. I payed my respect along with Meke and Tori. Then we exited the church.

Back at my apartment. I sat thinking about my future. I couldn't do nothing but reflect back on my past to get to where I was now in life. I had been raped by my mother's boyfriend when I was nine. Then DeWayne came into my life and gave me Sheria. Then Jay came into my life and got shot. After that, we had moved in together. Then came Martez. Now Kema.

Tank had died for the sake of defending my honor. I had paid my respect by going to his funeral and placing a set of flowers on his grave. But I was still searching for myself. I felt guilty at the moment about Tank's death. It was hard for me not to think about the night I was raped by the Blood gang members. And how Tank came to my room and promised he would get the guys back that raped me. I knew I had taken advantage of Tank. You can even say I manipulated him to kill those guys. Was I selfish? Yes, but those guys hurt me and I knew the police wouldn't have done nothing but give them a slap on the wrist for my pain. That's why I put my story together for Tank before he had arrived at the hotel the next morning after I was raped. I felt empty still from the rape and I felt like I lost a piece of my soul. Meke and Tori didn't understand the full detail of the beef between Tank and the Bloods. They didn't know Tank promised me he would get the guys that raped me.

MARTEZ

I had woken up feeling like I was about to die. My stomach felt like someone had taken a baseball bat and hit me with it. The night before I had been pouring liquor out for my childhood friend Chuckie. The Feds had come through and picked him and his crew up on Armed Robbery charges. Then came the news that shocked me the most. Tyron had been charged with the drug Rico act. He was in the Charlotte jail facing a life sentence on a king pin charge. His crew was picked up along with his muscle, Gemini. There wasn't really too much for me to worry about in the streets now. Tyron was gone so his beef with me no longer existed. Plus, Sam was cleared of all his drug charges after they had arrested Roy. The police had found Sam Jr in the care of a 60-year-old lady that stayed three blocks from Sam's store. Roy had paid the lady to care for the little boy while he continued to make Sam sell his product. When I found out that America's Most Wanted had viewed Roy's story on TV and a viewer had turned him in, I was a little relieved. It wasn't because he had gotten locked up, it was because little Sam was found alive. I knew I dodged a bullet when it came to Ty's case. The Feds could have put me in the 10-man indictment. I could have been facing 10 years in the joint too. But by the grace of God, he had watched over me. I knew I didn't have much longer to be selling drugs. My two-year run was almost over. I decided that I would go back to school once I got all my businesses off the ground. Now that I only needed to pay 10,000 to purchase this hole in a wall night club, I was ready to leave the game.

I didn't understand why someone would want to kill me. Then again, I was a major drug dealer in a up and coming city. Plus, I was having my way with any woman I wanted in the city. I had received several threats over the phone by an unidentified voice over the past few weeks. It was crazy during these two weeks because Tyron was in Charlottes Jail and the Bloods that I had fallen out with were dead or in the jailhouse too. I was still planning on how I would exit the drug game. There were still some loose ends that I needed to take care of before I could go into retirement. I had already invested in an ice cream truck, food stand, detailing shop, beauty shop, and a small night club on the East side of Charlotte. My deal with the club was still at a standstill due to the ten thousand dollars I was on my way to get from my grandmother's apartment. I didn't like to stash money at my grandmother's, but I knew this was my only safe place at the moment due to all the traffic and people that hung out around the middle section of my grandmother's apartment section. There were junkies and neighbors coming and going all the times of the day and the night. I came to the conclusion that if someone decided to rob my grandmother that it would be so many witnesses that someone would see something. Then, I could get revenge.

At the moment, everything was going as planned. No one knew about me using my grandmother's apartment as a stash spot. I had a decoy that no one paid attention too. Andrell was perfect for the job because her belly was big and this made it much easier for her to conceal the cash I was stashing at my grandmother's apartment. My grandmother knew everyone in the hood because she was the candy lady before I had started getting real money. There were times when her candy money was the only thing that kept our family above water. I appreciated my grandmother for her wisdom and knowing about the streets in general. She was a master mind when it came to fooling people. I guess I had gotten this trait from her because I use to watch how she would fool the people from the welfare department and the social service people when they came around to check on us. My grandmother respected my hustle but she didn't agree on me selling cocaine. She didn't like the fact that I could just quit school and jump off the porch head first in such mere corrupt way of life.

When I walked inside the common area of my grandmother's apartment, so many past memories took over. I could see all my old basketball and football accomplishments. There were shining gold and silver trophies on the large wooden stand that sat against the front wall. My grandmother was sitting on her leather back couch watching the news. She looked up at me when I made my way towards the stairway. She said. "Andrell called me the other night crying. "I turned around and said. "Don't pay her no attention."

My grandmother said. "That's the problem. You ain't giving that girl no attention. She told me about yall little episode. She threw your dope in the street?"

I made eye contact with my grandmother after I noticed she was wearing a house jacket, slippers, and a black scarf over her head. Then I said. "Andrell don't want for nothing. I buy her everything she wants."

"There are some stuff you just can't buy Martez." she said.

"Like what grand ma?"

"Like love and time." She said.

"I don't have time for this." I said.

"That's what's wrong with you. You never have time for no one but yourself." She said. I turned to walk off but my grandmother's words were cutting into my soul. I turned back around and said. "I think about you. You raised me. That's why I'm like that."

My grandmother stood up, and she walked slowly towards me. Then she stopped about two feet from my face. Then she said. "You made a choice to sell drugs. I didn't put no gun to your head and make you sell drugs. That was your choice."

"You think I like to sell drugs? You thing I like selling this stuff to people?" I asked. I slammed a gram of powder cocaine I had in my pocket on the table after my statement. My grandmother stared at this substance after it hit the glass table top. Then she said. "I can't tell that you don't like selling cocaine."

I shouted. "I don't! I only do it because I have too!"

My grandmother said "You don't have to. You do it because the money." Then my grandmother turned and grabbed the bag of money that I had Andrell stash in my grandmother's spare room. She tossed the bag at my feet and said. "That money got blood on it. Get it out of my sight." I could see in my grandmother's eyes that she was serious. It was like she was looking into my soul. I could feel the energy flowing from her eyes into my body. It was now tense in the room. If I didn't know better. I would have thought my grandmother was one of those junkies who I was selling dope too. I knew this was the beginning of my quarrel with my grandmother. There was no way I was getting out the door without her reminding me what cocaine had done to my father. She spoke. "You sell the same stuff your daddy likes to smoke."

"But I don't sell it to him." I said.

My grandmother said. "You still doing wrong. You out here selling that stuff to your own people. You killing the hood!"

I said "Do you think the rent man care about me selling dope? Do you think anyone in this hood care about me selling dope? I sell dope because I don't want to end up stuck in these projects waiting on food stamps and a check from the government." My grandmother stared at me like she was trying to kill me with her eyes. Before I could speak again, she cut me off. She said. "That's how you look at this neighborhood. You think everyone in this hood is waiting on food stamps and a welfare check from the government?"

My view of Dalton Village Projects and all the other projects in the world was the same. Most of the people that lived in the projects were on Welfare and received food stamps monthly. Growing up watching the news and living in these environments taught me that people living in these hoods were uneducated and lazy.

I came to the conclusion that if I wanted to remove myself from these surroundings, I had to do something to get out the hood. So, I decided to sell dope. Once I began to make money it was like I became addicted like a crack fiend. I answered my grandmother's questions. "Yes, I know most of the people in the hood is waiting on the government to take care of them."

My grandmother said. "You ain't no better. You sell to all these people that's getting these food stamps and welfare checks. You know two wrongs don't make a right." My grandmother was right in a sense. Two wrongs don't make a right, but the world dosen't wait on no one and I took this notion as my quest to get out the projects or be a product of my environment. As I made an attempt to pick up the bag of money and the gram of powder cocaine, my grandmother said "You gonna end up in prison or dead." I grabbed the bag of money after my grandmother threw that gram of powder cocaine at me. As I turned to leave, my grandmother pushed me in my back. I fell into the front door and the money spilled all over the entrance of the common area. I shouted. "Big Mama! I don't know what the hell is wrong with you." I attempted to put the money in the bag before my grandmother kicked the bag out of my hand. This sent a shock wave of anger through my body. I looked at my grandmother like

I could kill her. This was the woman that had my mother and I was now at the point of breaking all the principles that she had taught me when I was a child.

Before this day, I hadn't never dreamed or had a thought of putting my hands on my grandmother. I made an attempt to grab the bag to place the money back inside, but I was interrupted by a hard slap by my grandmother. Before she could react, I had pushed my grandmother to the ground. She hit her head on the floor. I heard the sound of police sirens as I picked up the bag again. My grandmother shouted "You know you shortening your days. You put your hands on your grandmother." My grandmother was known for going real religious on you, but to me she was the biggest fake religious person I knew. She had taught me how to lie and hustle at an early age. All the things she had taught me was now coming back in her face.

"You only live one life. It's up to you what you do with it." I said.

"That's why you gonna pay for your sins." She said. I took my grandmother's comment as another way of manipulating the situation. She knew I believed in God because this is what she had taught me to believe as a child.

"Well, we all gonna pay, but know one thing: I know I would rather be rich and pay than being broke and have to pay anyone." I said. My grandmother said "You so disrespectful Martez. You was hiding that money in my apartment. You didn't care if someone came here to kill me for that money."

My grandmother was crying now. She was really good at being dramatic.

"I paid you. Why do you think I gave you everything you asked for?" Then I started back picking up the money. I managed to get all the money back in the bag. Then, I grabbed the gram of powder and put it in my pocket. My grandmother said. "Det. Baily came her looking for you." I froze in my tracks. It had been weeks since Det. Baily tried to reach me. Somehow, he had got my cell phone number again and had managed to catch me. I told him that I didn't know the guys that shot Val, but Det. Baily was persistent with his work. He showed up at my dope spot on Farmer St., but I did not open the door.

"What did he want?" I asked.

"Now I got your attention," My grandmother said.

"Yea you got my attention."

My grandmother said. "He told me everything. Det Baily came here looking for you about the shooting that happened at your dope spot. He also told me that the Feds are looking into you."

I knew Det Baily was looking for me to show me the photo lineup of the guys that shot Val, but I didn't understand why he wanted me and Val was out of the hospital.

"What do he want with me?"

"He want you to be a witness when the Feds pick up the guys that shot Val. He said he could help you if you help him."

Grandma said. I was lost for words. It was like I was hit in the stomach with a bucket of bricks. I didn't understand how the Feds could pick up some guys for robbing crackheads until I thought about the law this crackhead Foots had explained to me one night while I was on the block. Foots schooled me how a Convicted Felon could be picked up by the Feds if he was caught with a gun. He had broken down the habitual offender law too. Due to the fact I haven't never been in the system, it was like he was getting me ready for the prison system. I knew there was a possibility that someone could snitch on me or set me up to be busted but I continued to chase that dollar bill. At the moment, I was an addict to them dead president.

I told my grandmother no thanks for Det Bailys offer. She said. "What about Andrell and the baby? I heard you got Nikki and another girl named Rhonda pregnant."

"I'm a man now, mama. When I left the nest, I became a man."

"Death or prison Martez." Then my grandmother continued

to cry as she watched me walk out the door. I felt numb, empty, and lost because I was now on my own in the world. There were even some feelings of bitterness and regret because I had put my hands on my grandmother, but her last two words touched something in my heart. Either I was going to get killed or go to prison for life.

EPILOGUE

MARTEZ

I never thought I would go to prison, but Det. Baily had always gotten his man. When I pled guilty to three years, I found out that it wasn't Gemini right hand man who I had shot in the back of my dope spot. Which brought me back to what my grandmother told me months before. The road I was on would lead to prison or death.

She was right, but life went on in which Andrell had "Qua Qua" a seven-pound little girl. I didn't get to be there when she was born but a week later Andrell and my mother showed up with Qua Qua Givens at my visit. Now, Rhonda was still with Jay living that lie. Some time you have to let people live life to find out the truth. I know one day Kema is going to look at herself in the mirror then look at Jay and realize that Jay isn't her father. Until that time comes, I will be waiting and maybe there will be a part two to this story. One last thing. Ty got life in Feds. Chuckie got 25 years, and Gemini got 30 years. Nikki and Keosha well that's another story.

RHONDA

I never thought I would turn to God for help, but all the stuff I went through as a kid and when I met Jay and Martez had taught me that I needed God. Now that Martez was in prison, I was feeling better about life. My secret was still a secret. Jay was still being Kema's father. Sometimes the person that birthed the child with the mother isn't the person for the job. Martez made me realize that life is too short to play games. He also taught me love is blind and it can take over your mind. Remember Mama's Baby Daddy's Maybe. One last thing. Vanessa and me are good friends now.

THE END.

PART 2
COMING SOON

A new saga begins…

Keep reading for a sneak peak of

TONY MONTANA

Coming soon!

PROLOGUE

Year: 1984
Place: Miami, FL
Early Summer
Following Tony Montana Sr's death…

Heartbroken by strife, Mrs. Clara Montana stood motionless in her small living room crying after she saw her son's face on the local evening news. The newscast reporter who covered the story went into great details about how Tony was Miami's biggest drug lord and concluded the story on how Tony had been gunned down, along with several of his men at his Montegro Beach mansion. The reason is unclear at this time. Possible warring cartel factions.

It had been two years since Ms. Montana had spoken to Tony. Her last encounter with him didn't go well. She could remember it like it was only yesterday.

"What are you doing at my doorstep, Tony?" she greeted him that day.

"I'm here to see Gina!" Tony has responded excitedly.

"Come Gina! Tony is at the door for you!" she announced loudly.

Gina came walking swiftly into the living room and while Ms. Montana looked on, Gina rushed into Tony's arms and after their greetings, Ms. Montana observed the conversation between the two.

Gina asked, "How long have you been in Miami, Tony?"

"Not long," Tony replied.

"You look good, Tony," Gina commented.

"I'm successful little sister. Your brother has made it to the big times and I have something for you," he said and then presented a diamond encrusted woman's necklace to her.

"It's beautiful, Tony!" Gina had said while she let him assist her with putting it around her neck.

After she got the necklace secured on, he handed her some

money.

"Thank you, Tony!" Gina had said and then looked at her mother.

The conversation took a quick turn after they entered the kitchen and took seats at the table.

"I'm in hair school, Tony!" Gina had said.

"That's good, Gina," he had said.

"I want you out my house, Tony! You aren't welcome here!" Ms. Montana said, in her quick demanding tone.

"Why, mama?" Gina had asked.

"Because he's a bum! I'm ashamed to say he's my son!" Ms. Montana said.

"Please, mama! Don't talk to Tony like that. He's your son!" Gina had said.

"You come around here dressed in your fancy clothes, jewelry, and throwing money around like you some type of big shot! You may impress Gina, but you're nothing but filth and I want you out my house. Right!! Now!!" she had yelled at Tony.

"Stop, mama!" Gina had shouted.

"What do you know, Gina, you're just a girl," Ms. Montana had said, waving her old wrinkled hand at Gina dismissively.

"Get out, Tony! Get out my house, now! Go!" she had said, pointing at the door.

"I have to go, Gina. I'll see you around," Tony had said as he headed towards the door.

"Don't ever come back here, Tony. You aren't welcome here anymore. And take your blood money with you," she said, as she snatched the wad of money out of Gina's hand and pushed it into Tony's hand.

"Now get out!" she demanded as she held the door open.

The sound of the car engine that was humming brought Ms. Montana back to reality. She walked over to the window and pulled the curtain back, and noticed the blue Buick in her driveway.

"He looks like a policeman," she said as she hesitated to go to the front door.

Standing at five-foot-three with dark hair, razor sharp eyes, and a young seventy-years old body, she had a low tolerance when it came to dealing with law enforcement officials. She had been physically abused by police in Cuba and her dislike and distain for them hadn't changed, but increased invariably ways when she had arrived in America.

A tall, slim built, white man stepped out of the vehicle, exposing his pale skin to the sun. Everything from his black suit, brown loafers and gun on his hip said that he was a cop.

"Please God, have mercy on me," Ms. Montana said as she grabbed a napkin off the living room table and wiped her eyes. She started towards the front door as she was looking out of the window at him. As he was reaching into the backseat for a brown box, his demeanor told her that the material inside the box was important. Her assumption was confirmed after he cradled the box like it was a baby.

When she arrived at the door, she put her ear up to the door and listened as he made his way on to the porch. The man's knuckles came next against the door.

She was startled by the knocking sound, but it didn't stop her from wanting to know what he wanted.

"Please God, don't let this be about Tony!" she whispered to herself as she turned the lock on the door and then swung it open. The man had his hand in the air like he was about to knock again.

"Who are you? And what do you want?" she questioned. Her demeanor was serious.

"First thing first, my name is Agent Terry Tadeo. I'm with the Special Drug Task Force Department."

She interrupted, "Get lost, I don't want to talk to you."

Then she made an attempt to shut the door, but Agent Tadeo blocked the effort by sticking his foot in the doorway.

"Ouch!" he shouted as the pain shot up his leg.

"I don't like police! I don't like police! Get away! Tony isn't here!" she shouted as she kept the pressure of the door on his foot.

"I'm not just here about Tony. My visit is about your daughter, Gina, too!" he shouted as he continued to struggle with his free foot.

"What about Gina?" she shouted as she still held the door.

"Gina is dead, Ms. Montana!" he responded.

The statement was like a sledgehammer. It sucked all of the air out of her chest. She let the door go and stepped away from it.

"Are you okay, Ms. Montana?" he asked as he slipped his foot from the doorway.

"Is Gina really dead?" she asked as she looked directly into his blue eyes.

"Yes. She was murdered at Tony's place," he replied.

"How? Why?" she asked in a whisper.

"Can I come inside the house?" he asked.

"No!" she yelled.

"I really need to talk to you about your daughter. I want to help find her killer," he said.

"Where is Gina's body?" she asked in a demanding tone.

"I really think you should let me come in so we can discuss this. Your life may be in danger!" he said.

Ms. Montana couldn't control her emotions and tears were forming in her eyes right before she yelled, "Just leave me alone. Get away from here!"

"Okay! Okay! Calm down. I'm leaving," he said.

The neighbors were watching now. Agent Tadeo placed the box on the doorstep and turned to leave and turned back around and said, "I'm sorry for your loss, Ms. Montana. But Tony is dead, too!"

She slammed the door in his face. "Well, that went well. All part of the job," he said and then stepped around the box and headed to the Buick.

She watched from the living room window as Agent Tadeo got back inside the driver seat of the Buick. She let go of the curtain when he looked in her direction. Then she took a moment to gather her thoughts as the sound of the Buick's engine took over the atmosphere. While backing out of the driveway, she could hear him shouting, "I'm leaving now, Ms. Montana. Sorry again!"

Seven months later…

Agent Tadeo had been sitting in his vehicle outside the Drug Task Force Headquarters, when he heard the dispatcher come over the air of the police scanner. The dispatcher said, "A woman had overdosed at a downtown hotel. We need units in that area." The hotel was two blocks over from where Agent Tadeo had been sitting in his vehicle. He drove over to the chaotic scene. A medical van was exiting the parking lot with a woman in the back of it. Agent Tadeo parked the Buick.

Then he hopped out of the Buick and walked over to the policeman that was in charge and who was also an old friend of his.

"Is the victim going to be okay, Jack?" Agent Tadeo asked.

"I'm not for sure, Terry," Jack said while he was writing out his report on his clipboard.

"Can you give me a run down on what happened here?" Agent Tadeo asked.

"Can't you see that I'm busy writing the report?" Jack said while he was looking up from the clipboard.

"I think this case could be linked to Tony's case," Agent Tadeo said.

"You still trying to find out who murdered Tony Montana?" Jack asked.

"Yes," Agent Tadeo replied.

"Well, this is going to knock your socks off! The victim is Tony's wife," Jack said.

"What?" Agent Tadeo responded.

Agent Tadeo was familiar with Tony's wife because of his investigation against Tony. She had helped him identify some of the players in Tony's world. This was why he thought that one of the players could be behind the overdose.

"Why are you so shocked? Everyone knows she was a coke head," Jack said.

"I'm not shocked. I'm just worried," Agent Tadeo said as he lit up a cigarette and took a pull from it.

"You shouldn't be worrying about her, Terry. It's our job to solve crimes, not to worry. Leave the worrying to the public," Jack said as he went back to writing his report.

"I have to get over to the hospital!" Agent Tadeo said.

"What, you got a thing for her?" Jack asked.

"No!" Agent Tadeo shouted.

"Well, why don't you leave this along and Tony's case, too," Jack suggested.

"I can't. Now I have to be going," Agent Tadeo responded.

"Where can I find you if anything comes up?" Jack asked.

"Over at the hospital. If you find anything that you think could help me, give me a call," Agent Tadeo answered.

"I have something you might not know about," Jack said.

"What is that?" Agent Tadeo asked.

"The Source is out on bond," Jack stated.

"How do you know?" Agent Tadeo asked.

"I have connections," Jack said.

"That's messed up," Agent Tadeo said.

"That's the American way," Jack retorted in a serious tone.

Thirty minutes later, Agent Tadeo pulled up in front of the hospital. The sliding doors to the emergency room opened, and he walked in the lobby to a chaotic scene. In the lobby was a couple with bandages on their heads, a man who had blood on his clothes, and a mother with a sick baby in her arms. They were all waiting for service.

After he flashed his badged and asked a nurse what room Mrs.

Montana was in, Agent Tadeo made his way to the third floor where an operating room was located. He stopped at the rim of the door and put his ear on it.

"We are going to need more blood for the patient and the baby. Get an IV ready for the baby. Hurry people, because time isn't on our side. The baby's head is wrapped around the umbilical cord and the blood isn't circulating properly in the baby's brain. The baby is under weight and has a very slim chance of surviving," the doctor shouted.

Agent Tadeo wanted to know the outcome of the operation, but was interrupted by a nurse as she pulled the door open from inside the operating room.

"What are you doing?" she asked.

"I was listening," he responded.

"Who are you?" she asked with concern in her tone.

"I'm Agent Tadeo," he replied.

"Are you family?" she asked.

"No," he said.

"Well, you need to go to the lobby," she said.

"I'm investigating the case," he said.

"What case?" she asked.

"The lady in there overdosed, right?" he asked.

"Yes. But right now, she can't talk because she's fighting for her life," she said.

A loud beeping sound took over the atmosphere.

"I have to go," the nurse shouted and then rushed back into the room.

Agent Tadeo knew the sound. He had heard it on many occasions while he was going other investigations at this same hospital. He knew from the sound that something was wrong. Very wrong! The evidence became transparent when he saw that more nurses were running down the hallway with breathing machines in their hands and two heart devices.

He was very familiar with death. He had seen hundreds of

people gunned down in the streets of Miami for drugs. Death was normal now. This was why he didn't inquire about Mrs. Montana when the nurses rolled her out on a gurney 30 minutes later. As he stood up, the nurse that he spoke with earlier said, "The mother didn't make it. They tried their best to get her to breathe, but she lost a lot of blood during the C-section."

"May I ask if the baby is okay?" Agent Tadeo asked.

"Yes, he is okay!" she responded.

"What is his name?" he questioned?

"Tony Montana Junior. The mother wanted him to be named after his father," she said.

"I'll be damned. Tony Montana Junior," Agent Tadeo said.

A new saga begins.

✦ 229 ✦

Keep reading for a sneak peak of
Ultimate Gang Coalition
Coming soon

PROLOGUE

Year: 2030

I was sitting inside my living room while I was playing around with my I-Phone when I received a video message and a file from my father. Instantly, I knew something was wrong when I looked into my father's brown eyes. As he spoke in a frantic-serious tone about the file that was labeled "ULTIMATE GANGS COALITION," my armpits started sweating in a perfusing manner from my nervousness. My heart had skipped a beat and I felt like I was about to go into shock.

At that very moment, I couldn't think straight, but I managed to transfer the file to a file drive on my phone like my father had instructed for me to do. After I destroyed everything in the house that could have let the police know that I had been communicating with my father, my next move was to get out of the house. I did this right before the FBI arrived.

I turned on my phone after I had hopped in my black 2030 Camaro GT Coup. Once on the highway, I checked the cameras at my house and I could see there were FBI Agents probing inside and outside of it. While they were searching, they found the little room that I had built under the basement where I had stored my father's belongings after he was sentenced to life in federal prison for a conviction of a terrorist act.

My sixth sense told me that I should alert Wiz about the raid, so I sent him a text as I exited the freeway and headed to West Blvd. When I reached Little Rock Road, I turned into Wiz's neighborhood and I could see that the FBI were already standing in front of Wiz's building. Instead of turning into his parking lot where the scene was extremely chaotic, I headed to a parking lot across the street from it. My heart was pounding so hard now that it felt like it was about to leap out of my chest. But I still wanted to investigate the scene, so I didn't let it bother me.

After I positioned the Camera in between a 2025 Mustang that was missing a headlight and a 2029 Ford Explorer, I disconnected the GPS system in my vehicle with the touch of a button. Next, I grabbed my phone and touched the screen and it went to the tint window feature. I touched it and the windows fused to darkness.

This feature was purchased to show off for the ladies, but at that moment it was helping me hide from the FBI. Since the Camaro was all black, even the rims, I felt like I was safe, but I wasn't. I could see that several FBI Agents were heading in my direction as I killed the engine. There was an AK-47 laying on the back seat. Was I supposed to go out like a street soldier? Or was I supposed to let the FBI get the file?

CHAPTER ONE

Year: 2029

Month: July

My name is Jihad Shakur. I was named after my grandfather to honor him for being a political activist. My father was just an infant when the FBI shot and killed my grandfather in front of my grandmother at their home on the west end of Chicago. This sent my grandmother running south, because she thought that the FBI would kill her next if she said anything about the murder. Due to her not speaking on the matter, the FBI spared her life and my father's life too.

My grandfather was a man that loved his race. He believed that the government was trying to kill off the black race through genocide, and he had formed this theory from studying different statistics of the black low-income neighborhoods. In his findings, he discovered that the government was using a statistical strategy to keep blacks in a low-state of life. The government was doing this by under-funding the public schools in the low-income areas, placing guns, drugs, and lead in these areas, too. Most kids in these areas were already counted as future criminals due to their environment. Most of these people didn't even know that they were victims of their circumstances and conditions.

Thank God for my grandfather, because I wouldn't have had the knowledge that I have if he hadn't formed a library inside his home before his death. In this library he had formed, he put all his knowledge about his findings in it. Plus, books about the government and how the CIA formed the internet and let others take credit for it.

My grandfather didn't attend public school or indulge in white man's ritual when it came to formal education. He schooled himself and others like himself. When he found out the CIA was tapping in to everyone's phone calls and TV screens, that was a no-brainer for him to go form his library. After reading my grandfather's article about "Government Spying," I came to the same conclusion he did. The government was spying on us.

This information was powerful around the time that my grandfather was killed. I can see now why they murdered him.

My father had inherited my grandfather's library after my grandfather passed away. He also inherited 2.5 million dollars that my grandmother had managed to keep hidden until her death. Right before my grandmother's passing, she asked my father to carry on with my grandfather's work. My father agreed, even though he knew he wasn't competent for the job. He had only agreed because my grandmother was on her death bed and he knew this was what she wanted to hear.

The first few months at "The Cure for the William Lynch Syndrome Organization," my father performed like a natural. But after he was getting heat from the media over an article that he wrote about genocide in the city of Chicago, my father walked away from the organization. He had left the organization in the hands of people that he thought he could trust, but it turned out that these people were moles from the government.

After my father left the organization, there were no more articles being written about genocide in America at the organization at all. The new owners of the organization changed the whole direction of the organization.

My grandfather had designed the organization to enlighten people about their state of minds and why they were in their perplexed states. He wanted to reverse their way of thinking by informing them about how William Lynch, a slave-master from the state of Virginia, had instructed other slaves masters how to instill hate in their slaves. My grandfather never got to see his movement come to full climax due to his death. But he did pass down the information to my father, in which my father passed it to me.

After reading over the information myself, I could see how the message of William Lynch was still working today. William's message taught how to divide and conquer. I could not see how blacks were stuck in this state of hating themselves and others because of William's message. This message had been passed down from generation to generation. And it was on the move to the next generation!

After learning about how my grandfather's organization was firebombed when he was running it, I decided to investigate on why he was murdered. In other words, why he was assassinated like Martin Luther King and Malcom X. He had power like those two great leaders and he wanted change for blacks just like them, and he also knew people had to die in order to get the equality that was due. That same due that was still lingering today, in which I've been called to bring forth such due.

I was named the "Chosen One" by my father, because he believes that I'm the person that can bring change for the gangs. And, bring down the government in the process. Do I think I can do it? I have some doubt. But I know if I work hard and have faith, I can change the world. My grandfather would think the same if he was alive. I just know it. I knew the government had put out false reports about my grandfather and father, and I found this out after I started an investigation into my grandfather's death. All the newspaper articles I had read about my grandfather told totally different stories about his death, that my grandmother had told me. She told me how my grandfather was classified as a threat to the government, and he was a threat because he was informing blacks on how the government was planning to enslave blacks by throwing them in prison.

My grandfather had been put on the FBI Most Wanted list because he declared that he was no citizen o the United States and his ties to the "UCC." He stopped paying his taxes and didn't use his social security number for anything. While I was looking over my grandfather's report about this, I found out that he didn't like the government at all. At first, I didn't understand all of his reasons why. But after learning how the government was living off the common people, the working people, and the low-income failures, I now have a better understanding of his reason. To this day, the government is still living off the blood, sweat, and tears of the American people.

My grandfather has never been a gang member, but he had ties to the "Black Panthers," and some of the gangs. I became a "Squad Lord" after my father became a board member on the Squad Lord's committee. Board members have a lot of power, and that power goes deep into the gang. I was just 12 years old when my father took me through the rituals, and since the Squad Lords gave my father his own branch, I gained rank quickly in his branch.

Now at the age of 25, I'm on the path of taking over my father's branch and more. My father had created a brand with his branch, and he had been selling t-shirts and other items to fund our movement before his arrest. He had even built a compound underground after watching tons of episodes of "Dooms Day," and he turned it over to the committee before he was arrested.

He believed that the government was planning to kill off a certain amount of people because the world was over-populated. I had taken on his belief after he had shown me his charts that contained evidence from the government's reports of crowded cities being harmed by deadly chemicals used in foods that were harming people. His theory was made off these reports.

I haven't seen my father since his 2008 trial, but I've talked with him on the phone.

Now that I'm in line to take over as head chief, some of the elders don't like it. And that have expressed their concerns, but their concerns don't concern me.

Today I have to meet with the committee. They will decide if I'm fit to take on my father's position. There are ten chiefs on the voting panel, and they are the main players in the gangs around the cities. I need at least six votes to become head chief. I think I will get them.

I hop in my 2030 Camaro and head straight to be best friend

Wiz's apartment. We both learned all the handshakes and the by-laws at the same time, and it wasn't an easy process. Wiz and I put our work in as foot soldiers too, and we earned our stripes.

When I pulled up in front of Wiz's building, he was standing out front of it. I hit the lock on the door and he hopped in.

"I can't believe your ass is early."

I responded, "It's best to be early than later."

He asked, "Are you ready to be a chief?"

"You know I am. I was breeded for this shit," I responded.

"Please don't change on me," Wiz said.

"You still going to be my right-hand Joe," I said.

"Cool," he responded.

CHAPTER TWO

Agent Tadeo

I'm Special Agent Terry Tadeo. I work for the United States government, which I'm part of the special Gang Task Force International team that was formed by the government to keep an eye on all gang members in the United States. I've been a part of this unit for ten years. I love my job, because it gives me a rush.

I made a name for myself by taking down Jihad Shakur Sr. He is an American Gang Terrorist that's currently being held at ADX prison in Colorado. He came up with a plan to unite all the gangs in American as one and to overthrow the government, and I arrested him and several members of his crew before they could execute their plans. I put several moles in their organization and I used recording devices that the moles planted in the building where their meetings were being held at to record them to build a case against them. I even got convictions on the top crew members in Shakur's gang. I save the tax payers' money by doing this.

The government has so many organizations that work together to keep this world safe. We take pride in our work, even though sometimes we have to break the law to get our men. It's part of the program, and we don't answer to anyone but the Attorney General. But he gives us enough rope to hang gang members as we see fit. So really, we don't answer to anyone. Not even him.

Our number one goal is to keep the government running by all means. If we have to steal, kill, and rob to do so, then we do. We do this so we keep the United States in order. That's why, when Jihad Sr. came up with a plan to overthrow the government, so we took him down. He was lucky that we didn't kill him, but he didn't cooperate. He spoiled our plan.

I drive up to the front entrance of the headquarters on the outskirts of the city. Standing in front of the Warehouse, that we call our headquarters, is my new partner, Brian Ray. I have a copy of his personal life file on my phone. He's been in law enforcement for ten years. 12 years less than me. He had joined the force after his sister was murdered by a gang member. I've seen his kind before. He's seeking revenge.

Brian is black and I'm white. That doesn't sit well with me. Most of my partners have been white; and the ones that weren't, I got them transferred to another section of the program. Brian gets in the passenger side of my 2029 Ford F-150. This service vehicle is solid black and it was issued to me several years ago.

He says, "I finally get to meet you in person."

"How the hell are you?" I responded.

"I'm fine as wine, sir," he says.

"You know about my history with black guys?" I ask.

"I've heard," he says.

"Well dismiss that notion. Today I'm taking on a new leaf," I respond.

"Why you say that?" he asks.

ABOUT THE AUTHOR

Qualo Lowery is from Charlotte, NC and he was born and raised there. He is single and working on another book along with a movie! He's been writing books since 2004. He has several books coming out soon!

Books by the Author:
Crumbling Talent
Queen City Mafia